MURDER IN THE FIELDS

A 1920S HISTORICAL COZY MYSTERY - AN EVIE
PARKER MYSTERY BOOK 18

SONIA PARIN

vJ23

ISBN: 9798396896871

1

Ripples in a day of rest

Sunday morning, the Village of Woodridge

*O*n this fine, late summer morning, the faithful were gathered together to give thanks, to receive spiritual guidance, and to rejoice with their fine and not so fine singing.

United, the parishioners' voices filled the little village church with joy and praise, and then fell silent to listen with respectful attention to the Reverend Jeremiah Stamford's sermon.

Everyone gave him their full attention.

Everyone except...

Evie nudged Toodles and, giving her a raised eyebrow

look, she issued a silent warning and hitched her head as if to suggest Toodles should pass on the elbow nudge, as well as the threat of dire consequences to Henrietta, who sat next to her, babbling away and expressing her opinions right in the middle of Sunday service.

"Do you really think she'll pay attention to me?" Toodles whispered. "Henrietta is intent on speaking her mind this morning more than any other morning. I doubt anything I say or do will stop her or even slow her down."

"Try," Evie urged, even as she strained to hear what Henrietta was saying about the new vicar.

"... *just impediment why these persons should not be joined together in Holy Matrimony...*"

"What did he say?" Henrietta whispered and must have nudged Toodles, who then nudged Evie and asked her if she had heard what the vicar had said.

"No, because I could only hear you and Henrietta... and Sara. Now, hush."

Henrietta leaned in and whispered her demand, "Well? What did she say?"

"She said to hush." Toodles jabbed Henrietta in the ribs.

"Was that absolutely necessary?" Before Toodles could reply, Henrietta hushed her. "He's talking again. I tell you, he has a squeaky voice, and it has nothing to do with my hearing. It reminds me of Mr. Jenson's cart," she mused. "He never oils the wheels and they squeak. When I was at the dower house I could always hear his approach, all the way from the other side of the village. It was quite notable because one wheel squeaked more than the other... What is he saying now?"

"He's still reading the banns," Sara whispered. "The

service should have ended by now. Just how many people are announcing their forthcoming nuptials?"

Someone else in the congregation entertained a similar thought.

It seemed the service would never end and they had so much to do. Everything had been timed to perfection. If the service didn't end soon, it would all be ruined.

What would happen then?

Would they have to find another weapon? It had been chosen with care but its use depended on the timing. Yes, the timing had to be right.

One blow to end it all.

"...*I publish the banns of marriage between Peter McCraw of Woodridge and Elizabeth Handicott of Woodridge. If any of you know cause or just impediment why these two persons should not be joined together in Holy Matrimony, ye are to declare it. This is the third time of asking.*"

Henrietta scoffed. "That's always sounded like an ultimatum. Don't you agree?" Deepening her voice, she said, "This is the second time of asking. This is the *third* time of asking. I feel like a child being scolded."

Sara concurred, "Yes. I'd never noticed before. I must say, that is a brilliant observation."

Toodles leaned toward Evie and, out of the corner of her mouth, whispered, "She does make a valid point. You'd think asking once would suffice."

Henrietta giggled. "He makes his squeaky voice sound solemn. That's quite a talent. I'll give him that. Do you think it's a nasal congestion?"

"He might have caught the cold you had last week," Toodles whispered. "You know, the one you passed on to me and Sara."

"I do not spread about germs. If you caught a cold, it was from someone else."

The elbow jabs worked their way along the front pew, up and down. Up and down.

Thankfully, they were silent during the closing prayer. However, as the congregation rose to their feet, Henrietta launched another string of observations about the new vicar, complaining about his constant fidgeting and his obvious fixation with only a couple of parishioners.

"I noticed that too," Sara declared. "I was expecting him to give you a warning look, but he didn't."

"Me?"

"You were the one doing most of the talking, and you're still doing it. I'm sure you haven't said half the things you wished to say."

Henrietta nodded. "He's too tall for me to see the top of his head, but I'm sure he has a bald patch covered by a longer strand of hair."

"And your point is?" Sara asked.

"Henrietta's point is not exactly appropriate in this setting," Toodles suggested.

"Well, I must agree. Perhaps I should wait until we arrive home." Henrietta smiled and greeted one of the parishioners, who hurried away, no doubt to discuss Henrietta's irreverent and incessant chatting during the service. Evie imagined it would be the talk of the village for the entire duration of the day.

My goodness, the Dowager Countess had a great deal to say in church today. Pass the salt, please...

Evie sensed Tom restraining himself. "I suppose

you're far too aware of our surroundings to make any comments."

Tilting his chin up, Tom smiled at her. "I'm on my Sunday best behavior, Countess."

"Yes, and I can't help thinking you're the one enjoying this the most. Henrietta's remarks are terribly unkind. The others are no better." Her voice hitched with a mixture of disbelief and annoyance. "I don't know what's come over them."

"Don't you?"

Evie snorted. "I suppose you know."

"It's a simple deduction, my dear. They were bedridden for days. Now they are feeling better and feel so revitalized they are making up for lost time."

Shaking her head, Evie composed herself and stepped out of the church and into the late summer sunshine. "Vicar. That was a lovely service. I found it very uplifting. Thank you."

Smiling, he inclined his head. "Thank you, Lady Woodridge."

As the vicar shifted his attention to Tom, Evie hastened to make the introductions, "This is Mr. Tom Winchester."

"I believe we've met."

Yes, they had met on two previous occasions and, both times, she had hurried to introduce Tom. All in an effort to avoid any misunderstandings.

They still had the matter of his knighthood to sort out before the situation became unavoidable and everyone started using his title. Far too many people read the notices, so, by now, it must have become common knowledge.

Tom was officially Sir Thomas Winchester.

It had been several weeks since Tom had been mistakenly awarded a full knighthood, instead of an honorary one, which would have made a world of difference as no one would have been required to use his honorary title.

Evie had acted with speed, contacting Sir Augustus Larson and he, in turn, had made discreet inquiries, bringing the matter to the attention of the Lord Chamberlain.

Sir Augustus Larson had told her it was a delicate matter. After all, the Warrant of Appointment had been signed by the monarch, who had then wielded the ceremonial sword, tapping Tom on the shoulders.

Evie hadn't known what to make of that. Forgetting everything she knew about ceremonial procedures, she wondered how one could undo the tapping of a ceremonial sword on a person's shoulders.

She wished it could be a simple matter of issuing some sort of retraction. Without asking, she knew Tom would happily spare the powers that be any embarrassment by accepting full responsibility for the misunderstanding. However, as Sir Augustus Larson had pointed out, this was a delicate matter. They had no option but to leave it all in his capable hands.

Tom and Evie walked on, making way for the rest of the congregation to stop and have a word with the vicar.

Glancing over her shoulder to see if the others were following, she saw Henrietta holding up the line.

"I should have stayed close to them to make sure they behaved," Evie murmured. She was too far to hear what was being said, but she trusted Henrietta to limit herself to a few polite comments.

Just as she was about to look away, Evie saw Henrietta drop a handkerchief, right in front of the vicar.

Of course, the Reverend Jeremiah Stamford, gentleman that he was, bent down to pick it up.

Evie groaned. "Unbelievable."

"What?" Tom asked and turned to see what had caused her reaction. Seeing what Henrietta had done, he said, "Never mind."

When the dowagers and Toodles caught up with them, Henrietta declared, "I was wrong, after all. He doesn't have a bald patch and a long strand of hair covering it. I don't know what made me think he did. Perhaps I allowed my imagination to run away with me."

Evie chastised her, "Henrietta, I think that remark was in very poor taste. I don't understand why you have made him a target. It's... it's very unlike you." When she had first joined the Woodridge family, Henrietta, the Dowager Countess of Woodridge, had been her beacon, offering reliable advice and assisting her in all areas of propriety. Without her guidance, Evie felt she would have been all out at sea, fumbling her way through a life replete with protocols foreign to her.

Henrietta blinked. "My goodness. I think I agree with you. There's just something very vain about the man. Am I the only one sensing it? How odd is that? And there's more, but I couldn't really tell you what else has caught my attention. I'm sure it will come to me."

Toodles snorted. "And you'll no doubt enlighten us."

"Of course. I wouldn't wish to leave you wavering in a sea of ignorance. What if what I'm sensing is a significant character flaw? We couldn't have that in our vicar. Not if it has a negative impact on our little community."

"Even so, that's no reason to..." Evie shook her head. "Never mind." She didn't wish to draw more attention to themselves or to kick up such a fuss on a Sunday, so she thought it best to drop the matter.

Tom hurried his step. Seeing his shoulders shaking, Evie knew he wanted to put some distance between them so he could finally laugh.

"I can hear you," she called out.

He reached the motor car and opened the door for her, his smile under control as he turned. "What? Did you say something?"

Rolling her eyes, Evie turned to the dowagers and Toodles who had reached the Duesenberg. "I'll see you back at the house."

As she walked away, she heard Henrietta say, "Oh, dear me, we're in trouble. Evangeline used her matriarchal tone."

Settling in the passenger seat, Evie straightened her skirt and muttered, "I do not have a matriarchal tone and... what does that even mean?"

"Countess." Tom drew her attention to the Duesenberg. "Edmonds has herded them in and they're on their way. You may breathe a sigh of relief."

Nodding, Evie took a moment to enjoy the silence, but she couldn't help interrupting it by asking, "I wonder if perhaps Dr. Weston misdiagnosed them. In particular, Henrietta."

Tom laughed under his breath. "No, I insist it's the bedrest and wholesome food. After days of suffering through the restrictions and being cosseted and overindulged by Mrs. Horace's cooking, they have now been restored to good health. I wouldn't be surprised to see them skipping and frolicking through the meadows, celebrating their new lease on life."

"That still doesn't explain or excuse Henrietta's behavior in church."

Tom laughed. "You're just worried you'll eventually follow in her footsteps."

Evie tipped her head back and groaned. "Yes, there's also that to consider..."

"Don't worry, Countess, I'll keep you sane."

"Thank you."

"Where to now? Home?" Tom asked.

"No, not quite yet." Evie signaled to the baskets secured in the rumble seat. "We have to drop those off. Then, home for luncheon and then..."

"And then we sneak out for our secret assignation?"

"That's the plan," Evie chirped.

Tom got them on their way, saying, "It was easy enough to keep a secret while they were bedridden. How long do you think it will take them to realize we're doing something behind their backs?"

"They're still too busy with the new vicar to pay any attention to us," Evie mused. "Actually, Henrietta's constant remarks are revealing a disturbing fixation with the poor man."

"Yes, what was that all about? Some of Henrietta's comments were downright... What is the word I'm searching for?"

"Juvenile?" Evie suggested.

"That's the one and it wasn't just Henrietta. They've banded together."

Thinking about Henrietta's remarks, Evie asked, "Do you think he's vain?"

"Who?" Tom asked.

"The new vicar."

"I haven't noticed. Is it a crime to be vain?"

"Henrietta seems to think so." Evie hummed. "I think they might have had one too many cups of medicinal rum and honey."

"But they're well over it by now."

Laughing, Evie asked, "Over their colds or the effects of the rum? For all we know, they might be taking precautionary measures and drinking rum for breakfast. This behavior is very unlike them. I'll admit Henrietta enjoys making her opinions known, but she is never unkind and is always the soul of discretion."

Could she really excuse their behavior as uncharacteristic? She'd known Henrietta to make the odd remark after a church service or social gathering, but Evie couldn't think of a single occasion, bar this one, when Henrietta had behaved like...

"Like a hoyden."

Tom leaned in. "What was that?"

"Nothing. Just thinking out loud." She signaled to the street ahead. "You need to make a turn there."

"Don't you usually invite the vicar to luncheon or dinner?" he asked as he slowed down and made the turn.

"Yes. I extended an invitation the first week he arrived. However, he was still settling in. So we agreed to postpone it. Then, everyone fell ill and... now... I'll have to delay it further. At least, until I know everyone will be on their best behavior."

"Pity," Tom murmured. "It would have been highly entertaining."

Leaning forward, she cast an admiring glance at the small garden filled with an abundance of flowers, including her favorite; delphinium. A light breeze swept through the little garden, sending the long-stemmed blooms into a joyful dance. "This is the house."

Tom brought the motor car to a stop and cast his gaze along the street. "This street doesn't look familiar. We should make the time to have a proper wander around and explore the village."

Agreeing, Evie turned and pointed to one of the baskets. "This one is for Mrs. Higgins." She went on to explain, "Mrs. Higgins is recovering from a nasty fall. I believe her ankle is still swollen, so it's difficult for her to get out and about. The other basket is for Mrs. Clarke. Her arthritis is playing up. It's quite sad because she enjoys being active and doing her own gardening. She also enjoys going around in her bicycle. I've seen her a couple of times and it always makes me feel we should get some bicycles."

"We?"

"Yes, it would be fun."

"When was the last time you rode a bicycle?" Tom asked.

Evie glanced away. "I can't exactly say, but I know you never forget how to ride one."

They walked up the little path leading to the front door, which they found standing slightly ajar.

"Is Mrs. Higgins expecting you?" Tom asked and set the basket down.

"Yes, I assume she is." Anyone who fell ill could

always expect a visit from someone at Halton House. "Oh, dear."

"What?"

She gestured toward the front door. "You tell me? Should we be suspicious of a door left standing ajar?"

In response, Tom asked, "Always expect the unexpected? You must admit, we have had our share of mishaps when we least expected them."

Evie's eyes widened slightly. "If we always expect the unexpected, then we would become suspicious of everything and everyone."

"Indeed," Tom agreed. "We'd always be on guard."

Evie cast her gaze around the pretty garden and felt glad it had been the first thing she'd noticed upon their arrival. How sad to always be looking for trouble and to always find fault and displeasure.

"Perhaps I need to adjust my thinking and make the unexpected the exception rather than the rule."

"Then, we should proceed with renewed confidence," Tom suggested.

Yet neither one moved.

Instead, they both leaned slightly forward and strained to hear something... anything that might alert them to trouble.

"Mrs. Higgins might have asked one of the neighbors to leave the door open," Evie suggested. "That's an acceptable explanation. Don't you agree?"

"A neighbor who came calling on her before heading off to Sunday service?" Tom asked.

"Yes, that sounds possible." Smiling, Evie looked heavenward. "Are we imagining a storm in a teacup?"

Tom looked up. After a minute, he asked, "Are you waiting for a response from the heavens?"

"Good grief. No. I think I always look up as a way to remove myself from a puzzling situation in the hope that I might find some clarity." Evie shrugged. "In any case, it's a trivial question, so I wouldn't really expect an answer. I'm sure the good Lord has better things to do than to get mixed up in matters of little importance."

A mewl had them both turning.

They both looked down and saw a cream and orange tabby sitting on the path, its tail flicking with impatience and its disapproving gaze directed at them.

"I think we might be standing in its way." Evie stepped aside and Tom followed her prompt.

The cream and orange tabby stuck its nose in the air and sauntered past them. Nudging the door, it waltzed right in.

"That will teach us to expect the worst."

Looking up, Tom hummed. "Perhaps nothing is too trivial for the powers that be."

Evie stepped forward and called out Mrs. Higgins' name.

"Do come in, please," Mrs. Higgins invited.

"Shall I wait out here?" Tom asked.

Evie shook her head. "I'm told Mrs. Higgins has been having trouble with her lights. She recently had the house wired and some of the lights have stopped working."

Tom tipped his hat back. Sounding puzzled, he asked, "And you assume I know everything about wiring and electric lights?"

"Of course, you're a man."

"And you trust me to be able to fix them?"

Evie beamed at him. "You've been a wildcatter, sinking exploratory oil wells. I'm sure that required some sort of mechanical know-how. This type of problem is right up your alley." It was Evie's turn to look puzzled. "You're supposed to know what to do about these things."

"You give me far greater credit than I deserve." He gestured toward the door. "After you, Countess."

"Don't forget the basket."

"How could I? It's right up my alley."

"Hello, Mrs. Higgins," Evie called out from the hall.

"I'm in the front drawing room, my lady. First door on your right."

As she turned toward the door, Evie heard someone rushing toward them.

Tom hurried to her side and drew her back just as a woman appeared, but he relaxed when he saw her drying her hands on an apron.

"I thought I heard someone at the door," the young woman said.

Mrs. Higgins called out, "That's my niece, Clara Dalgety. Clara, that's her ladyship."

The young woman blushed and returned their greeting, then excused herself and retreated to the kitchen.

They went through to the drawing room where they found Mrs. Higgins sitting by the window, her foot resting on a footstool. She thanked them for the basket and invited them to sit.

"You're much too kind, my lady."

"Not at all, Mrs. Higgins. It's the least we could do. And how are you feeling today?"

They chatted for a while and discussed the perils of

doing too much, especially when age required one to slow down. Although, Evie couldn't see her being much older than fifty.

"I really can't heal fast enough, my lady. My niece, Clara, has come to look after me even though she should be home looking after her sister, Margaret."

Evie expressed her concern. "Is she ill?"

Lowering her voice, Mrs. Higgins confided, "If you ask me, it's an old-fashioned case of melancholy. She and Clara lost their mother only a few years ago. She fell ill with the Spanish flu and never recovered. Margaret and Clara have been soldiering on but, every now and then, Margaret is struck by extreme sadness. It usually happens on the anniversary of my sister's passing, but that's not until later in the year."

Noticing Mrs. Higgins spirits sinking, Evie changed the subject. "I understand you've been having some trouble with your lights."

Mrs. Higgins told her all about it. "Funny little things, those incandescent bulbs. It's how I fell, trying to change one of those lights and, in the end, it was all for nothing because the bulb didn't work. I gave it a good shake to make sure everything was nice and tight."

Evie looked at Tom, who said, "I'm not sure shaking those bulbs is a good idea, Mrs. Higgins. The little wires come loose."

"Really? You'd think they'd make them sturdier."

"Would you like me to take a look?" he asked.

"Oh, would you? Yes, please. You're a tall fellow and the ceiling in the kitchen is low, but you might still need a step ladder. Ask Clara. She'll know where to look for it." She pointed toward the hall. "The kitchen is at the end.

Just follow the sounds of pots banging." Turning to Evie, she confided, "My niece, Clara, does the best she can, but she never uses a single pot if she can use a dozen. Margaret is the same. I would be there for her and, as soon as I am able, I will be. But Dr. Weston insists I rest for another week. Not that I'm complaining. Everyone has been ever so kind, dropping by for visits and bringing me baskets. Of course, none compare to yours, my lady. Mrs. Horace is a fine cook."

"I'll be sure to tell her you said so, Mrs. Higgins."

Mrs. Higgins glanced at the basket. "Her pies are particularly good. Everyone who's had a taste of them say so."

Evie smiled and assured her, "I think you will find one of them in there."

Brightening, Mrs. Higgins offered her some tea.

"That would be lovely. However, I'm afraid Mr. Winchester and I are rather pressed for time this morning."

Mrs. Higgins pointed to her ankle. "If not for this, I would be rushing off too. She came to visit me a couple of weeks ago. We went to Sunday service together and she stayed a week. She was in fine spirits, chatting and laughing."

It took Evie a moment to realize Mrs. Higgins was talking about her niece, Margaret.

Smiling, Mrs. Higgins' attention strayed to the window. "There's Mrs. Leeds. She's coming up the path. Bless her, she's been ever so kind. She always reserves the best blooms for Sunday service but she has been bringing me some lovely ones every other day to cheer me up."

Evie was about to offer to open the door, when she heard Mrs. Leeds letting herself in.

"Tessa, I was going to come this afternoon but then I saw Missy Higgins at my window. She mewled until I came out."

Leaning in, Mrs. Higgins whispered, "Missy Higgins is my cat. She's very helpful. Every time I mention Mrs. Leeds, off she goes to fetch her." Raising her voice, she said, "In here, Thelma. I have company."

Mrs. Thelma Leeds walked in, stopped and took a step back. "Good morning, my lady. Oh, dear. Perhaps I can come back later."

Evie greeted her and said she shouldn't go on her account as she would be leaving soon. "Those are lovely blooms, Mrs. Leeds."

Mrs. Higgins pointed to a vase and a jug of water. "I had Clara put those out on the table just in case you came to visit."

As Mrs. Leeds arranged the flowers, she must have forgotten about Evie's presence because she said, "I assume the vicar hasn't been to see you. I just saw him driving away in that smart motor of his. I might be old fashioned but it just doesn't look right for a vicar to be gallivanting about in something so inappropriate. Mark my word, it will be after midnight before he returns. The night before, the lights in the vicarage didn't come on until one in the morning. I was having one of my sleepless nights and sitting down to a cup of cocoa when I heard him and I looked out the window and sure enough, the lights in the vicarage came on."

To Evie's amusement, Mrs. Higgins did her best to catch Mrs. Leeds' attention, all to no avail.

"I put it down to his youth and him not having a wife," Mrs. Leeds continued. "There's just something that's not quite right about a vicar without a wife."

When she finished arranging the flowers, Mrs. Leeds turned and, noticing Evie, she blushed. "My apologies. Sometimes, I get carried away."

"It's not really gossip if it's true," Mrs. Higgins said.

Evie didn't want to own up to being surprised at the vicar. He had a duty to the parishioners and should have called on Mrs. Higgins by now.

Unfortunately, it would be up to her to have a word with him and that, she knew, wouldn't be an auspicious start to their relationship.

Needing to be fair, she decided to remain impartial. However, she couldn't help saying, "He is still new to the parish. Perhaps we should give him some time to settle in."

Mrs. Higgins grinned. "True. We can be a handful."

Oh, dear. Had she heard about Henrietta's behavior in church?

2

An unexpected visitor

*W*hen they were finally on their way to their next destination, Evie asked, "What took you so long?"

Tom tipped his hat back and glanced at Evie. "I actually finished fixing the lights a while back, but I heard you deep in conversation with Mrs. Higgins and someone else and I didn't want to interrupt you."

Evie fanned herself with a handkerchief. "I was hoping you'd rescue me. I've never encountered two women who can talk so much without having anything to say."

Evie tried to settle the whirlwind still tossing about in her mind. Mrs. Higgins and Mrs. Leeds had talked over each other. While their conversation had intermingled, neither one had missed a cue to answer or ask a question and she had been caught right in the middle of it all. "We need a special signal."

"A signal for what?" Tom asked.

"To alert each other."

"I'm still in the dark, Countess."

"We need something to let the other know their assistance is required. A word or a gesture. Something to prompt the other person to act with great speed and immediacy. And, before you suggest it, no, I won't employ a nervous twitch." As she spoke, Evie signaled to the street where Tom needed to make a turn. "We're looking for the house with a profusion of red roses. Mrs. Clarke is well known for her exquisite blooms, which always earn her a ribbon at the fair."

"If you introduced me to everyone in this village, I'm absolutely certain you would begin by saying, she or he is known for their beautiful blooms."

"Yes, most likely. You must admit, everyone here takes great pride in their gardens."

"Will Mrs. Clarke have incandescent bulbs requiring attention?"

"I believe one of the local villagers takes care of all the maintenance and gardening at her house. Although, she does most of the gardening herself."

"That's good to know, but if you'd warned me this morning, I would have hunted down a toolbox. Of course, now I will be better prepared for any future needs."

"If something needs desperate attention, we usually arrange for someone to come from Halton House. Today, it seemed easier to ask you. By the way, did Clara Dalgety say anything of interest?"

Tapping his fingers on the steering wheel, Tom said,

"She was preparing a soup and wanted to know if I'd seen her adding the salt because she couldn't remember. I suggested she taste it."

"And did she?"

"She did but only after adding more salt. Apparently, she was thinking about something else and became muddled. She actually yelped and jumped back from the stove saying she hadn't meant to add the salt until she'd tasted the soup. Then she blabbered about having too many thoughts whirling about."

"And?"

"I didn't dare ask about them for fear she might tell me all about her thoughts."

"I was asking about the soup, Tom."

He nodded. "It was too salty."

"Oh, dear."

Tom nudged her. "But I saved the day yet again."

"How so?"

"I suggested she put a potato in."

"And what does that do?"

"I have no idea but it seemed to do the trick. I don't even know where I heard about it." Tom chortled. "She must have panicked because she was about to drop a potato in the soup without first peeling it."

Evie imagined Tom had done his fair share of campfire cooking back in his wildcatter days. She also imagined Clara Dalgety had been slightly on edge. Tom was a handsome man and the kitchen must have been small enough for Clara to feel discomfited by the close proximity, or, at the very least, been quite aware of him.

"Did Clara Dalgety mention her sister? Mrs. Higgins had a lot to say about her niece, Margaret."

Tom nodded. Bringing the motor car to a stop in front of Mrs. Clarke's house, he sat back. "She said something about her condition only lasting until someone else caught her eye. But she didn't say what condition she was referring to and... no, I didn't ask."

"Until someone else caught her eye? Are you saying Margaret Dalgety is in love?" And, unrequited love, by the sounds of it, Evie thought.

"I'm sure this will not come as a surprise to you, Countess. I didn't actually ask. Remember, I was tackling the light bulb. However, I believe we can safely assume that's what she meant."

Evie snorted. "Admit it, you just weren't interested."

Tom smiled. "Yes, that too."

"If it's any comfort to you, Althea Rawlinson said her brother would be coming down this weekend to stay at the farm. You'll have some male company." Tom never complained, but she suspected he occasionally needed to spent time with other men, and talk about motor cars, fishing, and shooting.

They'd recently met Althea Rawlinson and her brother, who happened to be a detective. While Althea spent a great deal of time in town, both she and her brother made occasional trips to their farm located a short distance from Halton House.

"We shouldn't be too long. Mrs. Clarke spends her days reading and doesn't care for small talk or inter-ruptions."

"Does she have a niece?"

"I don't know. She might have. She will definitely be polite and she might even offer us some tea. However, mark my word, as soon as you set the basket down, she will start tapping her finger on the book she's reading."

A short while later...

As expected, their visit to Mrs. Clarke only lasted a few minutes. She had been reading the final chapter of a book and had been eager to get on with it because she'd been just as eager to start reading the next book.

As Tom drove along the winding road leading to Halton House and the house came into view, Evie mused, "I've never seen anyone cleaning the windows, and yet they always glimmer in the sunlight."

Tom laughed. "You've never seen me working on this engine, and yet the motor car always runs smoothly."

"Are you saying I need to stop and pay attention or just be glad everything is running like clockwork?"

Changing gears, Tom smiled. "Pick the answer that makes me look good."

"Here's a stray thought. I've heard say it takes an entire year to clean the windows at Blenheim Palace. Once the person in charge completes the task, he begins again."

"They employ a person just to clean the windows?"

"Yes." Evie brushed a finger along her chin. "I've never asked but it's quite possible the same happens here. Although, we don't have as many windows as the Duke of Marlborough's house."

"I hope you realize I will now remain curious until I

catch someone in the act of cleaning your windows." He glanced at Evie. "Are you feeling better?"

His question did not surprise her. It had been a trying day. "Yes, much better."

"Let's talk about something amusing," he suggested. "Something to keep your spirits up. I think half the problem here is that we take ourselves too seriously."

Evie was about to agree when, leaning forward, she pointed ahead. "I think we have company. I can see a motor car, but I don't recognize it."

"No, nor do I."

"Do you think it could be the vicar? Mrs. Leeds said he drives a smart motor car."

"So you *were* paying attention."

"I was caught in the crossfire. How could I avoid the conversation? I still can't understand how they kept up with each other. They each talked about something different."

As they drew nearer to the house, Tom shook his head. "I can see a chauffeur. Is the vicar driven around by a chauffeur? Surely, that would be too much for a vicar."

"Mrs. Leeds didn't say."

"Admit it, Countess. You didn't ask."

Evie tilted her head from side to side. "No, I didn't. I doubt I would have been able to fit a word in edgewise. Of course, I realize I should ask more questions and hone my observation skills. One never knows when some sort of tidbit might come in handy."

Evie's shoulders lowered. She had no idea what to expect from their visitor and could only hope they didn't ruin the rest of the day.

At that precise moment, she just wished to focus on enjoying the remainder of that lovely Sunday.

Evie cast her gaze around the surrounding landscape, taking in the manicured lawns around the house and the sloping hills beyond, with tall trees as far as the eye could see. She smiled at the clear blue sky with only a few slivers of clouds streaking across it. Yes, the day was simply too pretty to be spoiled.

"Whoever it is must be paying us a brief visit," she mused. "Otherwise, Edgar would have shown the chauffeur through to the kitchen. I still can't think who it might be. The motor is too smart for it to be a police vehicle. That's a relief. I'm rather enjoying having a break from criminal investigations." In the next breath, Evie realized their unexpected guest was being entertained by the dowagers and Toodles.

She could only hope Henrietta had recovered her composure.

"Have you slowed down?" she asked.

Tom glanced at her, his eyes glinting with amusement. "I thought it wise to proceed with caution."

"That reminds me," Evie said. "Earlier, when we arrived at Mrs. Higgins' house and heard someone approaching, you went to stand in front of me. What was that about?"

Tom lifted his chin. "We didn't exactly know what we were walking into. There might have been a knife wielding crazy person waiting to ambush us."

"Or an orange tabby with sharpened claws?" Although amused, Evie couldn't actually bring herself to laugh. They couldn't take any situation for granted, as they so often did.

Tom brought the motor car to a stop near the entrance. He climbed out and went around to open the passenger door. "Should we question the chauffeur?"

"I doubt we'll need to. Edgar has come out to greet us. I'm sure he is eager to report on this unexpected visitor. He's probably been hovering by one of the windows awaiting our return."

As Edgar was about to take the first step down, Holmes shot out of the house. Taking a giant leap over the steps, he startled Edgar, who tittered on the top step, his arms flapping about like a windmill. He recovered his balance just as Holmes landed on his front paws, tilted forward, performed a somersault and finally came to a stop in front of Evie and Tom.

Evie leaned down to pick him up and whispered, "You, Master Holmes, are a naughty dog. You could have caused Edgar serious harm."

Approaching them, Edgar greeted them. "You have a guest, my lady."

"Yes, we noticed and we are rather curious," Evie admitted.

Nodding, Tom said, "We've been trying to guess their identity. It's not the police." Tom leaned forward and lowered his voice. "Is it?"

"No, sir, it is not the police."

"That's a relief. Lady Woodridge and I have been enjoying the relative peace and quiet and don't feel ready to tackle an upheaval in our lives just yet."

"Tom," Evie whispered, "I know you're just trying to cheer me up but you mustn't tease Edgar."

Tom studied the chauffeured motor car. "It's a Rolls. It could be any number of people." He glanced at Evie.

"Your parents haven't come to visit you in a very long time."

Her parents?

That hadn't occurred to Evie. She had recently received a letter from her mother but there hadn't been any mention of a forthcoming visit.

Of course, she would need to issue an invitation soon...

"Why don't we let Edgar reveal to us the identity of our guest?"

"That's a splendid idea." Tom chortled. "Why didn't I think of that? You must excuse me, Edgar. I've had an interesting morning. Actually, we've both had a rather bizarre morning."

Evie hid her smile. "Oh... wait a minute. I think we presume too much. Perhaps the guest is here to visit Henrietta."

"Or Sara," Tom suggested.

"Or even Toodles." Before coming to visit and staying on, Toodles had traveled extensively. During her travels, she had met many people. "Then again, she might have mentioned something and I know she hasn't."

Tom's eyebrow hitched up. "I believe Edgar said *you* had a visitor."

"Yes, of course. We should let Edgar tell us."

Clearing his throat, the Halton House butler looked at Evie and then at Tom, almost as if testing to see if they had more to say. Satisfied he had their full attention, he announced, "Miss Phillipa Brady is here on an impromptu, whirlwind visit."

Tom and Evie both erupted, "Why didn't you say so?"

They both rushed past Edgar, with Tom saying, "This will definitely cheer you up, Countess."

"Yes, we haven't seen Phillipa in ages. Why do you think she's being driven around in a fancy chauffeured motor?"

Tom laughed. "Perhaps, as they say, she hit the big time and has come to bid us farewell."

"I wouldn't be surprised. Her plays have been met with wonderful acclaim."

Inside, Tom helped Evie out of her coat and Edgar reached them in time to take her hat.

"Where is she?" Evie asked.

"In the drawing room, my lady. The dowagers and Toodles are keeping her company."

"And why is her chauffeur still outside?"

"I'm not sure, my lady. I suspect Miss Phillipa was told you might not be back in time."

Evie hurried to the drawing room and was met by laughter.

"Evangeline. Just in time to talk Phillipa into joining us for luncheon."

"Phillipa! What a marvelous surprise." And, Evie thought, just what she needed to change the mood of that otherwise fine day.

The young playwright looked resplendently fashionable dressed in black wide legged trousers matched with a cropped jacket in vivid shades of purple, orange, green, and red.

"I hope you don't mind me dropping by unannounced." She grinned from ear to ear. "Did you see my fancy motor?"

"Yes. Edgar is going to show your chauffeur through

so he can have a proper lunch because, of course, you'll join us. I won't take no for an answer."

"Phillipa has been eager to share some news," Henrietta said. "And she insisted on waiting for you both."

"Does it have something to do with the chauffeur driven motor?" Evie asked.

"Yes, I've come up in the world." Phillipa beamed. "You'll never guess, so I'll tell you. My latest play is hitting the bright lights of Broadway. The producer is so keen, he has booked me on a first-class passage and provided the motor and chauffeur."

"Phillipa Brady is a star," Toodles declared.

"Congratulations and... my goodness, when are you leaving?"

"Tomorrow morning from Southampton. The producer has put me up at the fancy South Western Hotel."

Tomorrow! That meant she would need to set out for Southampton quite soon. "When did this happen? You should have told us earlier. We would have made a proper fuss about it."

"Yes, if we'd known sooner, we could have made a party of it. Oh, we might even have suggested traveling with you." Sara turned to Henrietta. "Think of the fun we might have had."

"I'm sorry I didn't tell you earlier but I only found out about it a couple of days ago. The producer is one of these exuberant people you don't dare say no to. He said, 'leave it all to me, honey,' and here I am bidding everyone farewell. I'm now feeling jittery because I realize we'll hardly have enough time, but I was hoping to get some news about your investigative activities. You know my play is about a house party murder." Phillipa gasped and interrupted herself, "I almost forgot to say, we very nearly didn't make it here in one piece and the experience has actually given me an idea for another play."

"What do you mean?" Evie exclaimed.

"A madman tried to drive us off the road. At least, that's what it looked like. My chauffeur had to perform some fancy maneuvering to keep us on the road. Otherwise, we would have ploughed straight into a tree."

"Heavens. What sort of motor car was it?"

"A roadster. Actually, a really nice piece of machinery."

Evie remembered Mrs. Leeds mentioning the vicar zipped about the place in a fancy motor and wondered if he had been responsible.

"I wouldn't be surprised if it was our vicar," Evie said.

"Why would you say that?" Sara asked.

Evie told them about their visit to Mrs. Higgins. "One of her neighbors dropped by and told us about the vicar whizzing around the place in his motor car."

"I suddenly feel justified in my observations," Henrietta said.

Evie wanted to tell her nothing could justify her behavior at Sunday service, but decided this wouldn't be the right time to bring up the subject.

"Do you think you could get a story out of the incident?" Toodles asked.

"I'm sure I can weave something together. It will give me something to do during the voyage."

Henrietta smiled. "Youth is wasted on the young. My dear, you are about to embark on an exciting voyage and you want to lock yourself away in a cabin writing a play?

Oh, there's another idea for you. Murder at sea. By the time you reach New York, you'll have another hit on your hands."

Edgar entered the drawing room and gave Evie a nod to indicate luncheon was ready.

Standing up, Evie said, "We're all very excited for you, Phillipa, and wish we could be there to see it all unfold."

They made their way to the dining room, with Phillipa saying, "Tell me more about this vicar of yours."

3

Secret assignation

Shortly after lunch

*B*y the end of the meal, Evie was celebrating the fact her day had taken a swift turn for the better. But then it was time to say farewell.

"My goodness, that was an unexpected and pleasant surprise," Toodles said as they waved Phillipa off. "Did anyone know this would happen?"

"It was bound to," Sara said. "Phillipa has a great deal of talent. I'm happy for her."

"Goodbyes always sadden me," Henrietta murmured. "But I'm too excited for Phillipa Brady to feel sad."

Sara sighed. "My social calendar is full for the next

few months. Otherwise, I'd be trailing after her. If only traveling didn't weary me so much."

They returned to the drawing room and sat down to reminisce about Phillipa, talking about their first encounters with her when she'd appeared in the village.

"Even if she didn't give us more time to organize a proper celebration, she at least thought to stop by before leaving," Henrietta mused. "Oh, I'm suddenly feeling rather bereft. I agree with Sara. It would have been quite exciting to join her."

Toodles stood up and was followed by the dowagers. They excused themselves saying they had letters to write, books to read, and walks to take.

Baffled by their swift exodus from the drawing room, Evie and Tom sat in silence for a good five minutes before Tom said, "What do you think that was about? Are they up to something?"

"They just want to take their minds off Phillipa's unexpected departure, Tom. We mustn't fear the worst. I think they might actually be mellowing and resuming their routines."

Tom's eyes glinted with amusement. "I will reserve judgment until next Sunday's service."

They took the footmen's entrance as a signal to make their way out to the hall. They had an appointment to keep. For several days now, they had managed to slip out of the house undetected. Eventually, they were bound to be questioned.

"Relief or disappointment. I can't decide which I feel." Not surprisingly, the dowagers and Toodles had used Phillipa's visit to divert all conversation during lunch away from their behavior at church that morning. Not that it would have been a suitable subject to discuss at that moment. But, somehow, they had managed to avoid it altogether.

"I'm guessing you are referring to our lunch?" Tom asked.

"Specifically, to the fact we avoided talking about the vicar and Henrietta's behavior. Right this minute, I think if we never hear another word about the vicar it will be too soon."

"When they exhausted their happiness and enthusiasm for Phillipa's good fortune, they must have discussed every single villagers' garden. I didn't know there were so many varieties of roses."

Evie nodded. "Relief. Yes, that's what I feel because I honestly don't think I could have discussed the matter with them."

Tom laughed. "They must be congratulating themselves on their lucky escape and plotting out their next escapade."

Looking toward the stairs, Evie mentally prepared herself for an encounter with Millicent. With Merrin still away, Millicent had been only too happy to continue acting as her lady's maid, and with no cases to tackle, she had been keeping herself busy organizing upcoming events at Halton House and had made a point of keeping her informed of all developments, leaving no detail out. "I'll only be two minutes." If she encountered Millicent, she would simply have to be firm and delay any discussions.

"Are you fetching a hat?" Tom asked.

"Yes, and I'm changing my dress."

"In two minutes? That will be a record. I'll be waiting outside."

Making her way up the stairs, she remembered Merrin was actually due to return from her extended trip that day. She imagined Merrin would have a lot of stories to tell, something Millicent would enjoy a great deal. So would she, but not right at that moment. If they wanted to be on time, they needed to leave right now.

Reaching her room, Evie eased the door open and didn't find anyone inside.

"Two minutes," she reminded herself. Selecting a hat, she checked her watch. "This will have to do."

As she rushed out of her room, she nearly collided with Millicent.

"Milady."

"My apologies, Millicent. I'm in a hurry."

"I just wanted to say I'll be sending Edmonds to the station to fetch Merrin..."

"She hasn't arrived yet?" Not waiting for an answer, Evie said, "Yes, very good idea, but tell me later. I really must dash."

Evie hurried down and out of the house and found Tom leaning against the roadster, his feet crossed at the ankles, his head tipped back to take in the afternoon sunshine.

"Two minutes, as promised," she declared.

"You're wearing the same dress."

"I'm sure I'm not."

"Yes, you were wearing a white dress with an embroidered central panel covered in tiny rose buds, and a sash with two small ribbons, barely noticeable, but there nonetheless. This is definitely the same dress. Or... one like it."

"And your point is?"

"We'll be late."

"That's your point?"

"Countess, we're going to be late."

Giving him a salute, she sat down in the passenger seat and, adjusting her hat, Evie peered up at the windows. "I don't see anyone watching us."

"If someone is watching, they'll soon lose sight of us." Tom put his foot down and raced out of the Halton estate.

Evie spent the drive to the next village thinking about Henrietta's behavior. It had been several weeks since they'd returned from town. Were the dowagers and Toodles missing the excitement?

After their return from town, one uneventful day had followed the other. They'd had nothing but sunshine and the usual lunches and dinners without anything going wrong. She and Tom had expressed their relief several times and hadn't once missed the excitement of investigating a case.

While she remained in business with Lotte Mannering, she had become more of a silent partner than an active detective. For now, at least. Evie knew that could change at any moment, as Lotte had already said there were some places she simply couldn't gain admittance to.

Meanwhile, she thought they should simply sit back and enjoy the relative peace and quiet.

Tom drove at a cracking pace, slowing down only when he saw a motor car approaching. The roads were so narrow in places, one or the other motor car had to pull over to let the other car drive through.

She was continually surprised he didn't impose himself on the road.

"Not really surprised," she murmured, only because she knew he couldn't hear her over the otherwise smooth rumble of the motor. Tom had a steady temper, betrayed only by his retorts, which were often quite witty. "And sarcastic."

Just as well there weren't that many vehicles traveling through these country roads.

A second later, another motor headed toward them.

At the last minute, Tom slowed down and steered the motor car to the shoulder, just barely avoiding a ditch.

With the other car driving through, Tom reclaimed the road and speeded up.

Evie watched the landscape whizz by. Turning her attention to the road ahead, she saw a motor car emerging from a treelined lane. It barely stopped before making the turn into the road and picking up speed fairly quickly.

Tom's jaw clenched and his fingers tightened around the steering wheel.

Narrowing her eyes, she identified the other motor car as a roadster. To her utter astonishment, it appeared to be hurtling toward them.

Evie braced herself.

She had complete trust in Tom's driving skills.

Evie snatched her hat off her head before it flew off.

Once again, Tom proved himself to be the bigger person by slowing down and giving the other motor car the right of way, but not without grumbling under his breath.

"Good heavens," Evie exclaimed. "That was the vicar."

"The man is a maniac," Tom muttered. Switching gears, he got them back on their way.

"I wonder what he was doing out here?" She didn't expect Tom to answer because she didn't think he'd heard her.

It wasn't until they'd arrived at their destination that she posed the question again.

"Maybe he had a secret assignation. Just like us." She wouldn't exactly call what they were doing an 'assignation', not even a tryst. Although, they were meeting one other person.

Tom slumped back in his seat and tipped his hat back.

Evie took a moment to steady herself. They were only halfway through the day and so much had happened. "So much for Sunday being the day of rest," she murmured as she climbed out of the motor car. Seeing Tom's expression of surprise, she shrugged. "You might as well know I don't always require you to open the door for me."

"I'm afraid I will have to insist. Otherwise, I'll be walking around with my hands clasped behind my back like one of those fellows who never has to do anything in life because it's always done for him."

Frowning, Evie looked into the distance.

That was enough to prompt Tom. "What?"

"I'm not surprised the vicar drives so fast. He certainly gets around. Earlier, he nearly ran Phillipa off the road. At least, we think it was him."

"Did she say where it happened?" Tom asked.

"I assume she came from London. Oh, that is strange. They would have crossed paths on the other side of the village. I stand by what I said. He gets around."

They walked up to the stately manor house. When Althea had referred to it as a farm, Evie had imagined a modest and rustic abode made of stone. This was anything but modest but it was made of stone and parts of it hailed all the way back to the Elizabethan era.

Before they reached the front door, it opened and the butler greeted them.

Evie returned the greeting, "Good afternoon, Withers."

"Lady Woodridge. Mr. Winchester." The butler inclined his head. "Miss Rawlinson is waiting for you."

"Is Señor Lopes with her?" Evie asked.

"He is indeed, my lady. Señor Martin de la Rosa Garcia Cortes y Lopes is in the library," Withers announced and led the way there.

Following him, Tom whispered, "Try saying that while standing on one foot. I bet anything Withers could do it."

As they approached the library, they heard the strains of the violin, followed by an accordion, piano and various other instruments.

They entered the library, which took up an entire wing of the house. Floor to ceiling oak bookcases lined one side. This was interrupted by a large stone fireplace in the middle of the room. In one corner, there was a spiral staircase leading up to the next level, which contained even more bookcases and a balcony running the full length. According to Althea, the collection had been established over a hundred years ago and the library had been an addition to the house that had stood for a lot longer than that.

On the other side of the room, there were tall

windows facing a private garden surrounded by tall
hedges with a gate providing the gardener access. Otherwise, it was a private haven.

Evie looked toward the fireplace and the sofas and
chairs surrounding it, and found Señor Lopes standing
by the fireplace, with his elbow casually resting on the
mantle, while Althea sat with her back to the door.

Hearing them enter, Althea swung around and stood
up. "Evie and Tom. We were beginning to worry you
wouldn't come."

Señor Lopes walked toward them, his back erect, his
chin lifted, a lock of his longer than was fashionable dark
hair falling across his eye.

His dark gaze fixed on Evie. Reaching her, he took her
hand and leaned down slightly until his lips hovered
above her knuckles. "Lady Woodridge, a pleasure to see
you again." His words were spoken in a thick Spanish
accent. Straightening, he looked at Tom and gave a stiff
nod. "Mr. Winchester."

Out of the corner of her eye, Evie saw Tom's eyebrow
lift as he acknowledged Señor Lopes. She hurried to say,
"Señor Lopes, I hope we haven't kept you waiting too
long."

"Not at all. Miss Rawlinson and I have entertained
ourselves with some music."

The tune they had been listening to came to an end.
Althea walked to the table where the gramophone sat
and lifted the needle.

Evie and Tom settled on the sofa, with Tom murmuring, "He held your hand for five seconds longer than
yesterday. Give him a week and he won't release your
hand at all."

Evie's eyes widened with surprise. "You timed him?"

The edge of his lip kicked up. "I entertained myself by counting the seconds."

"Tom, be nice. We need him."

"Shall we begin?" Señor Lopes invited.

An hour later...

After a productive hour, Señor Lopes thanked them for their attention and excused himself.

When the library door closed behind him, Althea offered them some refreshments. "Tea?"

Evie thought about the alternative. Returning to Halton House right at that moment did not appeal. Suddenly, she understood why Phillipa's departure had left Henrietta feeling bereft.

She would definitely welcome some excitement or a change of scenery, anything to distract her from that strange feeling of something missing.

Then, there was the other matter... If she returned home now, she would most likely have to deal with some sort of petty, unwanted problem. She supposed that would distract her but so would spending some time with Althea.

"Thank you. That would be lovely."

Althea rang for tea and settled opposite Tom and Evie.

"When is your brother arriving?" Evie asked.

"He said he was catching the late afternoon train so

he should be here in an hour or so." Smiling, Althea added, "I'm afraid our clandestine meetings are about to be exposed. I hope you don't mind."

"Not at all. It's all bound to come out soon enough. That's the whole point of the exercise. I have come to realize this business of secrecy doesn't suit me at all. I'm constantly on the lookout for anyone seeing us dashing off."

"Have the dowagers and your grandmother expressed curiosity?" Althea asked.

"No, they've been too involved in their own antics." Leaning forward, Evie added, "If Señor Lopes' presence causes any trouble for you, we should consider making other arrangements. Perhaps he could come and stay with us."

Althea dismissed her concerns. "Actually, he moved out of the house several days ago and insists on staying at the pub. He didn't give an explanation, but I suspect something or someone there has caught his attention. Did you notice how quickly he left after our business concluded?" Althea laughed. "Actually, I suspect his haste has something to do with Withers giving him disapproving looks." Althea shrugged. "Anyhow, Theo will find it all very odd but I doubt he will kick up a fuss. He said he was looking forward to a few days of doing absolutely nothing. So, nothing I do or say will stir him from that."

Tom smiled. "I would like to join him and do the same."

"You could do some fishing with him," Althea suggested. "There's a stream nearby. Poor Theo, I'm afraid I haven't told him about the dinner party I've organized.

Please tell me you're still coming. Theo will at least enjoy Tom's company."

Evie had nearly forgotten about it, and it was only a couple of days away. "Yes, of course. Tom and I are quite looking forward to it. Who else is coming?"

"A few local people including our neighbors, Sir George Gladstone and his daughter, Petronella, and a new acquaintance, Anna Bourke. She teaches at the local school."

The doors to the library opened and Withers walked in and set a tray down on a table.

"I'm dying for a cup of tea," Althea said. "Señor Lopes doesn't drink tea and seems to disapprove."

"Has he said anything about us making any progress?" Evie asked as she joined Althea and poured herself some tea.

Althea lowered her voice to say, "He thinks Tom is too rigid."

"Yes, he needs to relax," Evie admitted. "But I think he has the right attitude."

"What's that?" Tom asked as he came to stand beside her.

"You're full of enthusiasm and willing to embrace new ideas. That's Señor Lopes' opinion of you."

Tom snorted. "I've seen the way he looks at you. If we were still living in the age of dueling, I would have dragged him out of bed at dawn long ago and I believe he knows precisely how I feel."

"I had no idea you felt so strongly about it." Evie had noticed the occasional raised eyebrow, but she hadn't given it much thought other than to assume Tom didn't care for Señor Lopes' snappy instructions. Admittedly,

Señor Lopes softened his voice to a dulcet tone when he addressed her.

Althea changed the subject by asking, "Are you taking a break from working cases?"

Evie nodded. "Lotte has everything in hand. That's why we're doing this. Tom and I see it as acquiring new skills for our investigative ventures."

Althea snorted. "Somehow, I don't see Theo doing the same. When it comes to investigations, he's rather old school. But how do you hope this will help you?"

"Like any new skill, we believe it will allow us to look more credible." In reality, she and Tom were hoping to surprise everyone... when the time came. Evie lifted her teacup, only to lower it. "I never asked how you happened to meet him."

"I was delivering a portrait to the French Ambassador's wife. Señor Lopes had been their guest and he recognized me from the night I met you both at the Criterion."

"He was there?"

Althea nodded.

"What a strange coincidence."

"Yes, I suppose it is." Althea shrugged. "Anyhow, one thing led to another and..." she broke off. "Does his presence at the Criterion make you suspicious?"

"I don't see why it should. It's a popular venue."

Then again...

Before they'd left town, Althea had extended an open invitation to visit her at any time, which they had happily accepted, and she and Tom had met Señor Lopes on their first visit here.

"Countess? What is it?" Tom asked.

"I'm not sure..."

Señor Lopes had first seen Althea at the Criterion on the very night she and Tom had met her.

"Did you happen to mention to Señor Lopes where you lived?"

Althea gave it some thought. "Yes, I believe it came up in conversation."

"And did you give him an open invitation or were you specific about the date he should come to visit you?" Evie asked.

Althea closed her eyes for a moment and Evie imagined her thinking back to the day she'd met Señor Lopes. Being an artist, her mental image and memory of the day would be quite clear and detailed.

"He made some remarks about the English countryside. That's when I extended the invitation." She hummed under her breath. "Yes, I believe he was eager to come straightaway. He had been in town for a few weeks and needed to escape what he referred to as the madding crowd." Althea chortled. "That's odd. Now that I think about it, I believe he invited himself."

Tom and Evie exchange a look that spoke of interest.

Sounding concerned, Althea added, "He's a very good friend of the French Ambassador and his wife. I know they can vouch for him."

Evie set her at ease. "Don't mind me. Tom and I tend to be highly suspicious of anything that looks like a coincidence."

"I was going to say you must be enjoying taking a break but it doesn't really look as if you ever do."

Evie laughed. "What could possibly happen in this lovely corner of the world?"

Althea studied her for a moment. Lifting her cup of tea, the edge of her lip kicked up. "Indeed. However, I'd say you have just tempted fate."

A short while later...

Tom drove back at a cracking pace. Evie had no choice but to capture what she could of the landscape as it flew by.

On impulse, she drew his attention to a pretty field covered in wild flowers, not because she saw it coming up, but because she remembered it being just ahead from the many times they had driven past it.

Slowing down, he brought the motor car to a stop. "I take it you wish to delay our return to Halton House?"

"Heavens, no. What gave you that idea? I just wouldn't mind stretching my legs." Evie shrugged. "Actually, I'd like to try to enjoy what remains of this beautiful Sunday." Visiting Althea and carrying out their secret endeavor with Señor Lopes had already put her in a better mood. Right then, she decided she wouldn't bring up the subject of Henrietta's behavior at church.

Tom laughed. "You want to create a new memory to erase the earlier part of the day?"

"Something like that," she agreed. "Although, Phillipa's unexpected visit was lovely and I'm excited for her."

They climbed out of the motor. Tom helped her up a slight incline and they stopped to look around.

"Are we both looking for the same thing?" he asked.

"Most likely. For all we know, we wandered into a field with a feisty territorial bull."

"Nothing but wild flowers," Tom mused. "We'll be safe."

After a short walk, they reached a clearing. Evie stopped and tipped her head back.

"What is it?" Tom asked. "Before you ask why I'm curious, from where I'm standing you appear to be doing more than gazing up at the sky."

"I'm thinking about nothing in particular." She looked around and admired the pretty view of the undulating landscape. Thinking it would be a nice place to rest, she suggested taking a break. Tom stretched out on a clear patch of grass and she joined him. "Well... as a matter of fact, that's not exactly true."

"I'm not surprised. What's on your mind?"

"Did you find my curiosity about Señor Lopes strange?"

"No."

Evie laughed. "You'd say that because you, Mr. Winchester, are harboring a few biases."

"I might be and I must admit, your remarks have made me curious about him. He certainly doesn't strike me as the type to enjoy a lengthy stay in the country or even a brief one." Tom looked into the distance. "It must be all that Latin blood coursing through him. I see him as being more suited to the metropolis."

"You're right and, it is rather curious. Althea met him at the French Ambassador's house and that, of course, equates to a luxurious abode. Yet here he is, staying at a village pub."

"For all our suppositions and assumptions, that might actually be his natural habitat," Tom suggested.

"Perhaps. However, I don't understand why he wouldn't stay with the person who'd invited him here."

"Althea might be right about the butler disapproving of him. Every time I see Withers, I get the oddest impression he is still deciding what to make of me. Meanwhile, I am subjected to long measuring looks."

"You must be imagining it. Withers is ever so nice."

Tom snorted. "You don't have eyes on the back of your head. I'm sure I've seen him sneer at me as if I carry a bad smell."

"Getting back to the subject of our mysterious Señor Lopes, why do you think he rushed off so soon after we finished our business with him?"

"Are you annoyed at that and disappointed he didn't linger to enjoy your convivial company?"

"We haven't had the opportunity to become better acquainted. It seems rather odd. Especially as he expressed such an interest in coming to the country. You'd think he'd want to meet the local people."

"I see, you're annoyed because it disproves your suspicion."

"What do you mean?"

"He first encountered Althea at the Criterion on the same night we met her. Correct me if I'm wrong, I think you suspect he was drawn here by the notorious Countess of Woodridge. That can't be the case because, as you said, he rushed off and not just this time. He always leaves soon after our business is concluded. If he had been drawn here by you, he would linger after our meetings and, by now, he might have pushed to be invited to Halton House."

Evie played around with the scenario. Señor Lopes caught sight of her at the Criterion. A while later, he was staying at the French Ambassador's house when Althea walked in. He recognized her from the night at the Criterion and couldn't believe his luck...

Pushing out a breath, she sat up.

"Let me guess, you've been playing around with an idea and now you've hit a stumbling block."

"Yes, and I'm suddenly reminded of a game I used to play when I was a child. Whenever I finished reading a book, I would try to take the story further and imagine what else might happen. Or, in some cases, imagine what went on behind the scenes."

"And you're trying and failing to fill in the gaps about Señor Lopes?"

"Yes, and it's very annoying."

"A man of mystery."

"I hope he doesn't have an ulterior motive for being here." Shaking her head, Evie decided she wouldn't think about it anymore today. "Perhaps we should head back." She looked at her watch. "Heavens. We'll arrive just in time to change for dinner."

As they walked back to the roadster, she couldn't help bringing up the matter of Henrietta's behavior earlier that day. "Henrietta made an interesting observation about the vicar's attention being fixed on only three people. Did you notice that?"

"No, once she mentioned his squeaky voice, I became fixated with it."

"I'm no help. People appreciate being acknowledged

so I usually cast my eye around the congregation and smile and nod. On a normal day, I'd be able to tell you who was there and who wasn't."

Tom laughed. "But today you were wearing your matriarchal hat."

"That makes me sound dreadfully old." Evie huffed out a breath. "Althea would have remembered everyone who attended the service. Of course, she has the advantage of being a trained artist. Perhaps I should practice memorizing what I see."

"Don't ask me to participate because I still don't know everyone by name."

"But you'd be able to describe them," Evie suggested.

"Yes, I suppose so, and I actually see the benefit of the exercise. I'm sure the police would appreciate it."

"In case we ever have to give a statement?"

Tom nodded.

"We're bound to cross paths with the police again at some future date. Although, I'm in no hurry to do so. These last few days of relative peace and quiet have been blissful."

They reached the roadster and hesitated.

Tom laughed. "Are we dragging our feet?"

"I'm actually thinking about the vicar again and his fixation with only a few parishioners. I wonder what that's about. He's not shy. At least, not that I've noticed." He was relatively new to the parish. Evie had attended the last three services and, on the first two occasions, she hadn't been distracted by Henrietta and the others, yet she hadn't noticed anything unusual about his behavior.

"It's possible Henrietta might have been exaggerating," Tom suggested. "She was certainly wrong about his bald patch. In any case, I thought you'd given up trying to read too much into people's behavior."

"True. Let's make our way back. I'll spend the drive picturing a perfectly normal and uneventful dinner."

Meanwhile, observing from a safe distance...

Panic at the sight of the couple was replaced by relief when they left.

Plans were in motion and it was too late to back out now.

4

Another unexpected guest

Halton House

*T*om and Evie arrived just as Edgar was
sounding the dinner gong.

"One of the footmen saw you driving up, my lady.
Otherwise, I would have delayed dinner."

"Thank you, Edgar. We misjudged the distance and
the time. Although, Mr. Winchester did his best by
breaking all speed records." Sensing Edgar's disapproval,
Evie added, "Within reason, of course."

"Your new dinner suit has arrived, Mr. Winchester.
However, as you are expecting a guest tonight, I've laid
out your tails."

"A guest?" Evie exclaimed. She hadn't invited anyone. "Who's coming?"

"The Reverend Jeremiah Stamford, my lady. I thought you knew."

"No, I didn't." Had the vicar assumed she had issued an open invitation, one he could take up on a whim? It seemed so odd.

Edgar cleared his throat. Lowering his voice, he said, "I was informed by Lady Henrietta. I thought she might have been conveying a message from you."

"I see." She didn't really. She could only assume Henrietta had had a hand in extending the invitation, perhaps as a way to make up for her behavior earlier in the day.

"As I had no prior knowledge of this, I gave one of the footmen a half day off. I'm afraid we will be one footman short."

"I'm sure we'll manage, Edgar. Out of curiosity, when did Henrietta let you know?"

"This afternoon, my lady. She and Lady Sara went into the village. Upon their return, Lady Henrietta informed me of the vicar's visit."

"Toodles didn't go with them?" They were usually inseparable.

"No, my lady. I believe she was busy with her correspondence."

"Very well. Thank you, Edgar."

Making their way upstairs, Tom murmured, "I was looking forward to wearing my new dinner jacket instead of tails. Mark my word, the day will come when we abandon all these formal customs and adopt a more relaxed one."

Evie snorted. "Heavens, are you imagining sitting down to dinner in your regular suit?"

Tom's eyebrow hitched up. "You're not offended when I do that at luncheon."

"True. At least you're not suggesting dining with your shirtsleeves rolled up."

"No, I wouldn't go that far. However, now that you mention it..." He smiled and shook his head. "No, I don't suppose it will come to that. I'm sure even the game-keeper eats in his suit."

Evie rolled her eyes and headed for her bedroom to change. When she reached it, her hand hovered over the door handle, her thoughts on Henrietta. Had she mellowed or would dinner provide another opportunity for her to rebel and subject the vicar to who knew what?

"Just tell yourself the day will end on a good note," Evie murmured.

Shaking her head, she entered her room. Instead of finding Merrin, she found Millicent rushing about and talking to herself.

"Milady!"

"Millicent? Are you helping Merrin?"

"Oh... I assume Edgar didn't tell you."

"He told me about our unexpected dinner guest. Was there something else he needed to inform me about?"

Millicent gave a vigorous nod. "Merrin wasn't on the train, milady. Thinking we'd made a mistake with the date of arrival, I took the liberty of reading her letter again and..."

"And?"

"We were right to expect her today."

"It's possible she missed her train," Evie suggested as she sat down to remove her earrings.

So much for desiring an auspicious end to the day. She'd settle for humdrum, but even that seemed too much to expect.

"Edmonds had a word with the station master and he has agreed to pass on a message to telephone the house. That's just in case she does arrive on a later train." Millicent's voice quivered, "If she doesn't..."

Evie refused to be drawn into a state of panic. "Millicent, I'm sure there's a perfectly good explanation. She is very conscientious and wouldn't leave us to entertain a worst-case scenario."

"Milady..." Millicent hesitated. "W-what if someone snatched her? Only, one hears such stories about young women going missing. There are organized gangs. I hear they kidnap young women and sell them into slavery in faraway countries."

Evie tried to set her at ease but couldn't find any words that would convince her to calm down. Instead, she resorted to distracting Millicent with an account of her day, without revealing the secret she shared with Tom.

As Evie's tale unfolded, Millicent's eyes grew wider.

"Lady Henrietta said that... in church? And today, of all days, I decide not to attend..."

"That's unusual for you, Millicent. Weren't you feeling well?"

Millicent picked up the skirt Evie had just taken off and swung away. "I had a million and one things to do, milady."

"Millicent, have I been working you too hard?"

"No, you haven't. I just needed things to... be just right for when Merrin returned. I didn't want her to think I had let things go."

"You tidied up?" Evie laughed. "Only you would think of tidying before the maid came in to tidy up."

By the time she'd changed for dinner, Evie had told Millicent everything about her day.

Before making her way downstairs, she asked Millicent to keep her informed of any new developments and to make sure Edmonds would be available to collect Merrin if she arrived on a later train.

She met Tom at the foot of the stairs.

"What's wrong?" he asked. "You look as if you're carrying the weight of the world on your shoulders."

"This day can't end soon enough."

Tom laughed. "You say that as if whatever is troubling you will miraculously disappear by tomorrow."

"How very true, and I can only hope the problem resolves itself." Evie looked toward the drawing room. "Has our guest arrived?"

"Not that I'm aware of. The others are already in there and I only know that because I poked my head in. They're on their best behavior, hardly saying a word. I believe they will be quite tame tonight. Either that, or they're saving themselves for when the vicar arrives."

"Let's hope that's not the case."

"I might be wrong, but they have been rather quiet. I suspect they might have worn themselves out today. We could try crossing our fingers in the hope they'll be too weary to even comment on the weather. Cheer up, I'm sure tonight will be a great success."

Evie's shoulders lowered. "It might be best if I reserve

judgement until I turn in for the night. Let's go in before I lose my nerve."

Walking in, Evie noticed Toodles, Henrietta and Sara made no effort to disguise the fact they were all looking toward the door. Although, as she and Tom settled in a sofa, they became animated and overly concerned with adjusting their sleeves or skirts.

Accepting a drink from Edgar, Evie mused, "I believe we have a guest for dinner."

"Do we?" Henrietta looked intrigued. "Oh, yes. Of course, we do. That's why we were all so eager just now." She looked to the others for support but they chose that moment to turn their attentions to their drinks.

"It's strange..." Evie studied her glass and shrugged. "The vicar didn't say anything this morning."

A round of exchanged looks was followed by Henrietta saying, "It is rather strange." She turned to Sara. "Don't you agree?"

"Yes, yes, I do."

Evie glanced at Tom who looked equally perplexed. "You both went to the village this afternoon."

Henrietta's eyes brightened. "Oh, that was a lovely idea. When Sara proposed it, I must admit, it didn't appeal, but then she convinced me, saying we're headed toward the end of summer and the blooms will soon fade so we should..."

Sara nodded. "Yes, we absolutely had to. It seemed such a pity not to. It might all be gone tomorrow."

Since Evie knew they could keep up this nonsensical toing and froing all evening, she decided to shoot from the hip. "Henrietta, did you invite the vicar to dinner?"

Evie suspected the answer would come sometime around Christmas.

The room fell silent.

Evie almost gave up when Henrietta suddenly found her voice.

"Sara and I had been wondering if you'd forgotten to extend an invitation. In my day, the vicar was a regular guest at our table. It seemed strange that he hadn't been invited. In fact, Sara and I found it rather unusual and suddenly there he was. So we tackled the issue head-on. We must have both entertained the same idea because we both spoke at the same time."

"Yes, that was awkward," Sara said. "But I believe your voice prevailed over mine so, in actual fact, the invitation came from you."

"Did it? Well, in that case, it balances the books, so to speak. Yes, the invitation will have made up for my very bad behavior this morning."

"Henrietta thinks tonight will give her the opportunity to finally identify what it is about the vicar that has her... What was it you said earlier?" Sara asked.

Henrietta nodded. "Perplexed. We met one of the villagers, Mrs. Leeds, and she had a great many things to say about him."

"Mrs. Thelma Leeds?" Evie asked.

"Yes, she lives across the street from the vicarage and said he kept late hours. We thought we might find out what keeps him out so late. For all we know, he might suffer from insomnia, but that would be rather convenient. I am more inclined to think there is another reason and it involves nightly escapades. He might not even be a vicar. What do we actually know about the man?" Henrietta looked at Evie and then at Tom. "You both possess a criminal turn of mind. Haven't you sensed something odd about him?"

Evie hadn't given it any thought. Since his arrival, she'd only seen him during the church services she'd attended. The first time she'd met him she'd extended an invitation. On the other two occasions, she'd only had a brief word with him after the service. The rest of the time, she and Tom had been busy entertaining guests. She might have given the matter some thought if she'd actually noticed something out of place about him. But she hadn't.

Shrugging, Tom admitted, "Nothing's caught my attention."

"That proves it," Henrietta declared. "He is a master of disguise and subterfuge."

Good heavens, how had Henrietta reached that conclusion and why did she seem intent on finding something wrong with the vicar?

Evie dreaded to think what tactics Henrietta would employ to extricate the information from him.

Noticing Toodles lost in her own thoughts and wishing to change the subject, she asked, "And how was your afternoon, Granny?"

"My correspondence kept me entertained. Your cousins will be receiving some lovely letters from me soon. They think I don't know they've taken up residence in my apartment."

"An apartment?" Henrietta looked mystified.

"I believe you call them flats."

"Oh, I see. I thought you had a house," Henrietta remarked.

"That's in Newport and, over there, we call those types of houses cottages. I was referring to the New York apartment." Toodles' eyes brightened. "On the wrong side of the park."

If Henrietta took the bait, she did not show it. "I'm not sure what that means. In fact, everything you said mystifies me. I've heard you describe your Newport house and it sounds quite grand and yet you call it a cottage. Anyone would think there is something in the water you drink. As to your apartment being on the wrong side of the park... Well, is there such a thing? And I'm sure I heard you mention your house on the Upper something or other."

"I have a house on the Upper East Side, as one does, but that is for show. A while back, I secured an apartment at the Dakota and kept it all under wraps."

"Because it's on the wrong side of the park?" Henrietta asked.

"Some people think that. I prefer to see it as the lively side of town. Anyhow, it's where all the interesting people live."

"And now your granddaughters have taken up residence?"

"By stealth," Toodles said and looked toward the door. "When is the vicar going to arrive?"

Half an hour later, they were still waiting for the vicar and they had exhausted all the safe subjects of conversation.

"Perhaps he's been called away," Sara suggested.

Henrietta didn't seem to think so. "Why? He's not a doctor. Oh, do you think he might have been called on to give comfort to someone about to take their last breath?"

Sara shuddered. "You don't suppose something

happened to him along the way. Mrs. Leeds told us he drives like a veritable maniac."

"Yes, I can attest to that," Tom said.

"I'm sure we would have heard something by now," Evie suggested. "The village is within walking distance of Halton House. If anything happened to him along the way, he would have returned to the vicarage, and he would have sent word."

As Henrietta and Sara looked toward the door, Evie's gaze lowered. The day had been long and she had hoped to put it all behind her with an uneventful meal.

Lost in her thoughts, she missed seeing a footman approaching Edgar and holding a hurried conversation with him. However, when Edgar cleared his throat, she looked up.

"My lady." Edgar stood near the door looking alarmed. At least, as alarmed as Edgar could ever look. His eyes had widened slightly and he had forgotten to give his sleeves a tug.

"Yes, Edgar. What is it?"

Stepping forward, he visibly swallowed. "The footman, Anthony, has just returned early from the village. If you recall, I had given him the evening off. He says the village is... Well, it's alive with intrigue."

"What do you mean? Has something happened?" And, she wondered, did it involve the vicar?

"No one seems to know exactly. Anthony lingered for as long as possible. Sirens were heard in the distance and he personally saw a police vehicle drive through the village at great speed."

That could only mean something had happened just beyond the village.

Evie shifted to the edge of her seat. Tom set his drink down and rose to his feet.

Evie didn't want to think the vicar was in any way involved. She set her own drink down and stood up. "Edgar, could you ask Edmonds to drive to the village and speak with Mrs. Leeds. She lives across the street from the vicarage and might have some information. She seems to be well informed about the vicar's comings and goings."

"Very well, my lady. What should I do about dinner?"

Toodles stood up. "We can't let good food go to waste. I'm sure it's too early to panic and lose our appetites."

Henrietta looked at Evie, her eyes wide with surprise. "Do you think the vicar is somehow involved in this so-called intrigue?"

"Henrietta, I'd prefer not to jump to conclusions. However, he was supposed to be here and he isn't."

Ten minutes later, Edgar returned to say dinner was ready and to confirm her ladyship's instructions had been carried out.

They all followed Evie into the dining room. As they had expected the vicar to arrive, a place had been set for him. Taking their places at the table, they sat in silence looking at the vacant chair.

Henrietta spoke first. "Rather than jump to conclusions and think something dreadful has happened to the vicar I'm going to suggest he has been called in to assist with administering spiritual guidance."

"Yes," Sara agreed. "Or he might have been waylaid. If he was making his way here, Edmonds will most likely encounter him along the way. Toodles is right. It seems such a shame to let a good meal go to waste. Let's change the subject. Otherwise, we risk giving ourselves indigestion."

Henrietta laughed. "My goodness, Sara. You've thought of everything. It almost sounds as if you had a contingency plan ready and waiting to be used."

"I always have one. It's called common sense and is the best weapon to use against utter nonsense. I suggest we put any talk of the vicar to rest."

Everyone enjoyed the first course, their intermittent chatter forced as they all struggled to avoid mentioning the vicar. However, by the time the main course was served, it had become quite obvious the vicar would not be joining them and, as everyone's attention kept drifting to the empty chair, it was also quite obvious they were all wondering what had happened to him.

Edgar walked around the table serving the wine. When he reached Evie, she asked, "I suppose there's no point in asking if Edmonds has returned."

"You will be the first to know when he does, my lady. I have one of the footmen waiting by the front door looking out for him."

"He should have returned by now." Henrietta looked around the table. "Do you think he has gone in search of information beyond whatever Mrs. Leeds could provide? I daresay, he wouldn't want to return empty-handed. That would be a dreadful anticlimax. Poor Edmonds, I should hate to be in his shoes. He must know we depend on him to deliver reliable news. It's not difficult to imagine him taking the task on as a challenge and setting his sights on a triumphant return."

"Henrietta, you sound as if you are trivializing what could well turn out to be a serious outcome."

"Sara, at my age, one must cast light on all matters and diminish their impact. Wherever possible, one simply must take precautions. I have spent my life staying out of the sun, avoiding its detrimental effects on my skin. Worry can be just as harmful." Henrietta leaned in and narrowed her eyes. "Might I suggest you do the same. The light in this room is casting some doubt on the condition of your skin."

The door to the dining room opened and a footman entered. He looked around. When he located Edgar, he signaled to him. After a brief exchange, Edgar turned to them and hesitated.

"What is it, Edgar?"

"It's the vicar, my lady."

"Oh, thank goodness, he's here." Henrietta took a sip of wine. "Just in time to enjoy dessert."

"I believe his condition would prevent him from doing that, my lady," Edgar said.

Henrietta's gaze bounced around the table. "What on earth is that supposed to mean? Has he been taken ill?"

"No, my lady. He has simply been taken."

Evie intervened, "Edgar, ask Edmonds to come in, please."

"I'm afraid I cannot do that, my lady. Edmonds returned to deliver the message and has set off again. He said he wanted to drive out to see for himself. I'm sorry, but that is all I know. The message was given to a footman."

Evie turned toward the windows. Being summer, the sun set a lot later than usual. However, surely there wouldn't be enough light for Edmonds to see by.

"Would someone please explain what is happening and are we getting our pudding tonight?"

"Henrietta." Sara rolled her eyes. "The vicar is dead."

Taken aback, Henrietta's eyes widened. "When did that happen?"

"That's just it. We don't know and now Edmonds has driven out to find out more," Evie explained.

Henrietta murmured, "The vicar might have let us know before we spent an evening worrying about him."

Toodles gave her a look of incredulity. "I doubt the man knew he was going to die."

"You can't know that for sure. He is... was a vicar." Henrietta looked up. "He was in dialogue with the man upstairs."

"What are you going to do?" Sara asked Evie.

"Me?"

"You'll have to investigate," Sara explained.

"Without knowing how he died? You assume his death was suspicious." Evie looked at Tom. "We only ever become involved if we happen to notice something that doesn't quite make sense or look right. Besides, we don't have confirmation."

"It must be him," Henrietta declared. "The man isn't here for dinner. Where else might he be? Before anyone challenges my reasoning, it is perfectly acceptable and, I might add, sane. And, if he isn't dead..." Henrietta nodded, "Evangeline, you will still have to investigate. Find out all you can about the man. One way or another, I must know what it was about him that bothered me so much."

Evie frowned. "You never said you were bothered by him."

"Oh, dear. Did I not make myself clear this morning?" Henrietta looked up. "And where is my pudding?"

The drawing room

Evie was surprised Tom did not choose to stay behind to enjoy a brandy and cigar in his own company.

"I wanted to," he said, almost as if he had read her mind. "But I didn't dare abandon you."

"You're just trying to garner points with me."

"Yes, that too." He tilted his head and studied Evie for a moment. "Actually, do I need to? Yes, I suppose it doesn't hurt to squirrel away points." He shrugged. "In case of a future transgression."

"Still no news, my lady," Edgar said as he served the brandy.

Did she have reason to worry?

"Edmonds must be taking his scouting mission with the seriousness it deserves," Tom mused. "He must know we want absolute proof of the vicar's demise."

How had he discovered the news? The footman had claimed the village had been full of intrigue. That could mean anything from everyone reacting to the news, to everyone entertaining their own theory about the presence of the police.

"Edgar, please find out what time Anthony saw the police car drive through the village."

"Certainly, my lady."

As he turned to leave, Henrietta said, "Edgar, do

please send my compliments to Mrs. Horace. Her pudding was magnificent and well worth the anticipation and wait."

Inclining his head, Edgar said, "Mrs. Horace will be delighted to hear you said so, my lady."

That seemed to surprise Henrietta. "Edgar, do you mean to say Mrs. Horace doesn't know we appreciate her delightful food? Have we been remiss in not expressing our appreciation? Do please assure her we love her cooking."

Edgar inclined his head again. "Very well, my lady."

As he stepped out of the drawing room, the chatter resumed. One by one, they glanced at the clock on the mantle, almost as if to witness the passing of time.

Evie pondered the strangeness of sitting in comfort and safety while chaos whirled around somewhere not far away. That led her to think about choices. Sooner or later, they would have all the facts at hand and they would have to decide how to proceed.

Would she and Tom become involved? She knew the police would resolve the matter as expediently as possible. If a crime had been committed, they would get to the bottom of it.

But what of the rest?

Henrietta had already pointed out the fact they knew very little about the vicar. What would they discover if they delved into his life?

Toodles took an appreciative sip of her brandy before saying, "Well, I came here out of curiosity to see how Birdie was getting on with her life, and I stayed for the excitement and entertainment. I cannot say I have been disappointed."

Henrietta tittered. "I should like to take some credit for your satisfaction."

Toodles lifted her glass. "Of course, you have done a marvelous job of leading me astray."

Edgar returned, his face grim as he spoke, "My lady, Anthony says he saw the police motor drive through the village three hours ago. He lingered in the village, hoping to get some news. It seems everyone had a different theory."

"I'm not surprised. Does he know if there are any actual witnesses? Perhaps someone driving by as the police stopped or made a turn."

"No, my lady."

"Well, I hope Edmonds has better luck." Of course, that meant waiting for news. Reliable news, she thought.

"It must feel odd to be sitting here while someone else is out and about searching for answers," Henrietta observed.

"Not at all. It makes for a nice change of pace. A sort of reversal of roles." And, if the news turned out to be bad, she would have the opportunity of employing a different tactic.

She and Tom had been the first on the scene too many times to count. She'd never stopped to think about it, however, now she realized she'd never shied away from the crime scenes. If she had been an avid reader of murder mysteries, her interest could be justified. In reality, she preferred to immerse herself in a book about any subject other than fiction.

"For all we know, this is nothing more than a road accident."

"Evangeline, the police have been called in. This must be a dreadful accident."

Even so, Evie thought it would be better than eventually learning someone had met their end under suspicious circumstances.

This was definitely too close to home. One didn't really wish to entertain ideas of a murder being committed by someone they'd seen in the village going about their business every day.

Someone they knew.

Someone they trusted.

"I shudder to think what this might mean." Henrietta drew Edgar's attention to her empty glass.

"You could try thinking of something other than the worst-case scenario," Toodles suggested. "Think what it will do to your complexion."

"Oh, heavens. I hadn't considered that."

"In your place, I would finish that drink and say goodnight. Tuck yourself in with a good book. Perhaps a romantic novel."

"Retire for the evening? Without first learning what Edmonds has discovered? I'm afraid this has already taken root in my mind. It would be impossible for me to convince myself to wait until the morning."

Toodles laughed. "Are you afraid of losing an argument with yourself?"

Henrietta nodded. "I can be a fierce objector and I dare not take sides."

"So there are three of you in there? It must get crowded."

Henrietta looked smug. "It does indeed when I have my own audience."

A footman entered and had a brief word with Edgar. They then stepped out of the drawing room.

No one spoke. Instead, they all sat up and looked toward the door.

Evie heard a murmured conversation followed by footsteps, which stopped outside the drawing room.

The door opened and Edgar entered. "My lady, there are two constables asking to speak with you."

"Evangeline?" Henrietta looked intrigued. "Is there something we should know? You and Tom were absent from the house this afternoon..."

"They are probably canvassing the area, Henrietta." That could only mean the incident took place fairly close to the village.

Evie stood up and was joined by Tom.

When they reached the door, Evie realized the others were following them.

"I would rather hear the news first hand," Henrietta said.

Toodles agreed with a nod. "Me too."

"But surely we can't all follow," Henrietta reasoned. "Perhaps you and Sara can stay and I'll tell you all about it."

Toodles rejected the plea. "Your versions have become unreliable."

"What?" Henrietta demanded. "To think how much effort I put in, always delivering a colorful account."

"And therein lies the problem. You overdramatize your version."

Sara agreed. "You can't deny it, Henrietta. I've seen you practicing in front of a mirror. You pay particular attention to your hand gestures, using them to interpret your emotions."

Henrietta lifted her chin. "To quote Shakespeare, all the world's a stage, and all the men and women merely players. I don't wish to go to my grave thinking I haven't played my part. You two have some catching up to do."

Unsettling news

*E*veryone walked out of the drawing room and were met by the sound of raised voices.

Two constables stood toe to toe with Edgar.

"I merely informed her ladyship of your presence. How dare you accuse me of, as you say, giving her ladyship a heads up. I have a good mind to force you to take your muddy shoes and your bad manners, and wait outside."

"Now, see here, who do you think you are?" one of the constables demanded.

"I am her ladyship's butler and you will not take one more step inside this house unless invited to do so by her ladyship. In her place, I would certainly not extend such a courtesy."

Edgar's chin lifted while the constables puffed out

their chests and narrowed their eyes into deep, truculent scowls.

Tom whispered, "I'm tempted to draw you back just to see what happens next."

"Oh, heavens. You've just read my mind." Squaring her shoulders, Evie approached the group.

One of the constables, the most sensible one, Evie thought, turned toward her. Stepping forward, he fractured the tension that had threatened to erupt.

"Lady Woodridge?"

"Yes. How can I help you?"

"We have a man in custody. He claims to work for you."

"Indeed, and what is the man's name?" she asked, even though she knew he had to be referring to Edmonds.

"He says he's your chauffeur, Edmonds. He wouldn't give us his full name."

Just as well, Evie thought, because she didn't know Edmonds' Christian name. To her, he'd always been Edmonds. "And where is he now?"

"He has been handcuffed and is outside."

Evie tried to remain calm but she made sure to express her disapproval by hitching her voice. "Handcuffed? Why?"

"We caught him at the scene of a crime."

Evie had no qualms about revealing her involvement. "He was there at my request."

"So you can confirm his identity."

"I can do that if you release him and bring him inside."

He glanced over at the other constable who appeared to be more interested in locking horns with Edgar.

"Constable, unless you have a legitimate reason for holding Edmonds in custody, I'm afraid I will have to insist you release him immediately," Evie declared, her demand made with many reservations.

She had never intervened in a policeman's duty and, despite her involvement in several cases, she had never imposed her will on any officer of the law.

Right that minute, she wished to speak with Edmonds so she could establish the full facts. She didn't believe he had, in any way, interfered with the police investigation and she didn't understand why the police officers had felt compelled to arrest him.

"Very well. If you say he is your chauffeur, we will release him." He tugged his colleague's sleeve twice. Responding with a nod, the other policeman gave Edgar a visible sneer.

Evie waited for them to step out of the house before saying, "Edgar, I hope they weren't too difficult."

"Not at all, my lady. I believe I have the advantage of being underestimated."

That didn't surprise her. Most butlers she met were rather mature, some almost ready for retirement. Edgar was in his thirties. Only she knew that, before coming to work for her, he had been in the army. Benefiting from a well-to-do distant relative, he had started as an Officer Cadet and had risen to the rank of Lieutenant. For reasons only known to him, he had left the army, going into service and swiftly rising to the position of butler. When war had broken out, he had returned to the army. She had never questioned him about his experiences during the Great War and was only too glad he had managed to come through it all unscathed.

"Evangeline, that might have been you in handcuffs."

"What do you mean, Henrietta?"

"You and Tom often find yourselves in the middle of a crime scene. You sent Edmonds out to investigate, but I'm sure your first instinct was to set out with Tom and see what the fuss was about. I suspect we had something to do with you remaining here."

Toodles snorted. "You credit yourself with saving Birdie from the embarrassment of being arrested?"

The edge of Henrietta's lip lifted. "I believe I included you and Sara. You can both share the credit for keeping Evangeline out of trouble."

"Now you seem to be excluding yourself." Toodles snorted again. "I'm willing to bet anything Birdie stayed put because she didn't want to leave you behind to create who knows what chaos."

Henrietta pressed a hand to her chest. "Me?"

Sara nodded. "You have been an instigator and, some might even say, agitator today. Actually, I might even go so far as to say you were a bad influence."

"Me?"

Rolling her eyes, Toodles turned to Evie. "Well, this hullabaloo can't be about the vicar being killed. Who would want to kill a vicar?"

Henrietta frowned at Toodles, before saying, "But the village is full of intrigue. The villagers are not easily stirred. Certainly not on a Sunday. So there must be some truth to the rumor."

"Yes," Evie agreed. "But until we hear some real news, it will all remain a rumor."

Edgar drew Evie's attention to the door. "They are returning, my lady."

When Evie saw Edmonds, she gasped. "Good heavens! What happened to you?"

Edmonds looked the worst for wear. His trouser leg had a rip. His tie sat askew. His hair looked ruffled and his shirt appeared to be smeared with dirt.

"He resisted arrest," one of the constables explained.

Edmonds grinned. "They manhandled me first and asked questions later, my lady."

Feeling incensed, Evie declared, "I shall be speaking to your superiors."

Shrugging, the less abrasive constable drew out a notebook and pen. "So you can confirm Edmonds was at the scene of the crime at your request."

"Indeed, I can." Her eyebrows drew down. "I still don't understand why he was apprehended."

"Some criminals return to the scene of the crime and pretend to be spectators," the constable explained.

"Yes, I'm well aware of that theory but the criminals usually lose themselves among a crowd. Where exactly did you apprehend my chauffeur?"

"He was lurking by the side of the road near the turn off leading to the scene of the crime."

"You mean to say he kept a respectable distance and did not get in anyone's way?"

The constable closed the notebook and tucked it inside his pocket. "The entire area is an active crime scene. For all we know, he disturbed vital information. There might have been footprints."

"Judging by the way his clothes have been muddied, I

assume you tackled him to the ground and I'm sure that did not help."

The constable gave a firm nod. "Please make sure your chauffeur stays well away from the scene. We do not need spectators. Consider yourselves warned. This time, we will not press charges."

Henrietta stepped forward. "Young man, I hope you realize you have just issued a warning to the Countess of Woodridge. If her ladyship doesn't lodge a complaint with your superiors, I certainly will for endangering the life of our chauffeur and failing to show due reverence. I would not treat my gardener with such a lack of respect."

"I'll be sure to let them know they should expect to hear from you," the constable bit back.

Henrietta huffed and appeared to be once again caught with no appropriate retort. Meanwhile, the constables swung on their feet and walked out.

Shaking her head, she murmured, "I think today has worn me out."

Toodles wove her arm through hers and patted her hand. "It's very late in the evening, Henrietta. At your age, you can't expect to provide a sharp comeback retort at the drop of a hat. He should consider himself lucky he didn't catch you this morning."

Evie turned to Edmonds. "I'm so sorry I sent you out there."

"Not at all, my lady." Edmonds grinned. "I was more than happy to go out and investigate on your behalf and, when it came to it, I gave as good as I got. I should consider myself lucky not to be charged with assaulting an officer of the law."

"Would you like to freshen up and then join us in the drawing room?"

She was about to ask Edgar to organize a meal for Edmonds but saw him by the front door appearing to keep an eye on the departing police officers.

Evie heard the motor car drive away. However, as Edgar was about to close the door, he hesitated.

Evie took a step forward. "Edgar?"

"There is another motor car approaching, my lady."

Everyone took a step forward.

"Who on earth could it be at this time of the night?" Evie murmured.

"The killer?" Henrietta suggested. "In which case, Edgar should be slamming the door and bolting it." Henrietta looked around the hall, her gaze skipping from a display of antique swords to several ancient firearms lined alongside the fireplace. "At the very least, we should arm ourselves with..."

"An eighteenth-century dwelling pistol?" Toodles suggested. "Or a sparring sword?"

"My dear, you might not know this but I am an excellent swordswoman." Henrietta thrust her finger out for effect.

"Why doesn't that surprise me?"

Evie stepped forward again. Glancing over her shoulder, she saw Tom keeping up with her.

"Before you ask, I have no idea, Countess." He looked at his watch and nodded. "It is late for visitors."

Edgar stepped out, his pace determined. Evie heard the crunch of gravel and a motor car coming to a stop. A murmured conversation ensued but was beyond her hearing and succeeded in adding to the tension building around her shoulders.

A man entered and her mind must have played tricks on her because she didn't immediately recognize him. Instead of proceeding inside, he stopped and turned to hand Edgar his hat and coat.

Another brief exchange followed and, as the man turned, Tom said, "*Henry*?"

Evie gaped.

Lord Evans?

Caro's husband. Here?

"Henry," Evie exclaimed. Looking beyond his shoulder, she searched for Caro even though, in her mind, she knew Caro could not have accompanied him. Otherwise, she would have been the first through the door, her arms outstretched, her smile wide as she announced her arrival.

Good heavens. Had something happened?

No, she swiftly convinced herself all was fine.

Lord Evans, otherwise known as Detective Inspector Henry Evans, was here on official business. He had to be.

Greeting them, he gave Evie a worried smile. "I'm afraid I will be throwing myself at your mercy. There are no rooms available at the pub and—"

Thinking that if something had happened to Caro, he would have said so by now, Evie interrupted him, "You are always welcome at Halton House. I assume you've brought luggage."

"Yes. I didn't wish to presume so I left it in the motor."

Evie gave Edgar a nod. A footman appeared and followed him out to get the luggage.

"Come through. We were just about to have some

coffee in the drawing room. Have you dined? If you haven't, I can organize a meal for you."

"Thank you. I had something at the pub."

The dowagers and Toodles sat together on a sofa and watched with interest and in uncharacteristic silence. Evie assumed they were giving her the opportunity to speak first.

"How is dear Caro?"

"She is very well and will be surprised when I tell her I came here."

So Caro didn't know he was here. Evie assumed Henry Evans had been sent to investigate the incident, but she now had to again wonder if something else might have brought him here.

Oh, dear. She hoped he hadn't come to issue another warning. Once before, he'd tried to steer Caro away from becoming involved in investigations. Of course, Caro had taken exception to his interference and objections and Henry had been forced to do some serious groveling.

"I suppose you've heard the news," he said.

Evie admitted, "We've heard some rumors about an incident and I sent Edmonds out to investigate."

Henry Evans smiled. "And what did he discover?"

"We haven't had a chance to speak with him. He only just returned but will be joining us soon."

Henrietta spoke up, "He was handcuffed and roughed up."

Henry Evans appeared to be genuinely surprised by this. "Roughed up? By whom?"

"By a couple of constables," Henrietta answered innocently.

"We don't know the full details," Evie explained.

"They were just doing their jobs and making sure the crime scene was not disturbed. Edmonds appears to be quite amused by it all."

Tom cleared his throat. When Evie looked at him, he nudged his head toward Henry Evans.

Evie drew in a breath. "We're actually eager to hear some sort of confirmation."

"If it wasn't such a serious matter, I'd be tempted to suggest we wait for Edmonds." Henry Evans clasped his hands and gave a firm nod. "The local vicar was found dead in a field not far from the village."

The vicar? Dead?

Evie's response to the news surprised her. They had been talking of nothing else and, when they'd fallen silent, she was sure they'd all been thinking of nothing else.

"Did you say he was found in a field?" Tom asked.

Henry Evans nodded.

Her mind immediately fixed on that afternoon. She and Tom had interrupted their return by stopping for a while to walk through a pretty field and enjoy a moment of peace and quiet.

Her mind crowded with a dozen questions. As she looked around the drawing room, she saw the dowagers and Toodles staring into space, their eyes wide with surprise.

Dozens of questions barged into her mind. Selecting one at random, Evie asked, "Who discovered the body?"

Henry Evans did not hesitate. "A young woman. She was on her way home."

Evie tried to picture the scene but failed. Most of the fields near the village were raised slightly higher than the road. In order to access the field that afternoon, she and Tom had clambered up a slight incline.

If the young woman had been walking home, what had prompted her to divert her journey?

Evie accepted a drink from the footman, although she had no intention of drinking it yet as she needed a clear head. "The body was visible from the road?"

"No."

Henry Evans had surprised Evie by saying as much as he had. Indeed, she was surprised he hadn't changed the subject. He actually seemed more than willing to discuss the death. Although, the alternative would have been to lie about the reason for his visit.

She waited for him to say more and realized that he might be willing to share information but she would have to work hard at encouraging him to reveal more.

"Did she wander into the field?"

Henry Evans nodded.

The dowagers and Toodles all shifted in their seats, a sign they were all eager to ask questions.

He glanced at them and, before any of them could speak, he said, "The young woman wanted to collect some wild flowers."

And out of all the fields in the county, she had stumbled upon one with a dead body?

Evie thought she heard Tom whisper, "Bizarre."

She met his gaze and wondered what other thoughts he might be entertaining and was soon enlightened.

"What's her name?" Tom asked.

Henry Evans dug inside his coat pocket and produced a small notebook. "Elizabeth Handicott."

The name sounded familiar.

The dowagers exchanged puzzled looks, with Henrietta saying, "I'm sure I recognize the name. I just can't think where I heard it mentioned."

"Yes, I think I'm familiar with the name but I can't place it," Tom agreed.

Henrietta's eyes skipped around from one person to the other. Evie could tell she wanted to say something else but she hesitated, either because she'd already said enough that day or because she wasn't entirely sure what she wanted to say.

Finally, Henrietta spoke up. "Lord Evans. How did the vicar die?"

"Henry, please."

Of course. Evie shook her head as she realized it hadn't occurred to ask the most basic question.

"Shouldn't you be addressing him as Inspector Evans?" Sara asked. "After all, he is investigating a case."

Since it was the first time Henrietta had addressed him, it seemed quite fitting that she should use his title, Evie thought. However, in this instance, he wasn't really Lord Evans. He had come on official business.

"Detective Inspector Evans," Toodles corrected.

Overruling everyone, Tom asked, "Henry, how did the vicar die?"

"A severe blow to the back of his head."

The dowagers and Toodles leaned back and gasped.

"I knew there was something strange about him. He was up to something," Henrietta said. "And someone killed him because of it."

"Yes, but what was he up to, Henrietta?" Toodles asked.

Henrietta's eyes widened in surprise. "I suppose we

will never know now." She glanced at Evie. "Of course, Evangeline could get to the bottom of it."

"Birdie? Investigate?" Toodles laughed. "You seem to forget Detective Inspector Evans is here to investigate the matter."

"You're right, of course. Evangeline will have to work by stealth and not tread on his toes." Henrietta turned to Henry Evans. "Do you have any suspects?"

He tried to hide his smile as he answered, "No suspects and no motive. Although, his wallet was missing."

"You think this is a robbery gone wrong?" Evie had trouble believing that.

"It's too early to say with any certainty. However, if I had to lodge a report now, the missing wallet would be my only piece of supporting evidence."

"So this is not just a social call. You really are investigating." Henrietta gave a decisive nod. "In that case, you will want to speak with us."

"And why is that, Lady Henrietta?"

"Because we attended Sunday service and everything the vicar did and said struck me as odd. We witnessed it all. I'm sure that if you question the congregation, they will all have a thing or two to say about the vicar. He's been in this village for only three weeks and, if I hadn't been ill, I'm sure I would have questioned his character much sooner. Unfortunately, I was bedridden for the most part."

"I'm sorry to hear that, Lady Henrietta. How are you feeling now?"

"Much better, thank you."

Evie lifted her glass of brandy to her lips, her

thoughts fixed on the woman who'd found the vicar. "You said Elizabeth Handicott stopped to collect some wild flowers. Did she go there for that particular purpose?"

Henry Evans regarded Evie for a moment, long enough for Henrietta to murmur, "Evangeline has asked a key question. The entire case might be solved on the basis of something that hadn't even occurred to the police."

Sara elbowed her and gestured toward Henry Evans.

"My dear, I'm sure the detective can take some minor constructive criticism. My remark was a mere observation."

"In answer to your question, I couldn't really say." He glanced at Henrietta. "Yes, I will make a point of asking her. I do, however know Elizabeth Handicott had been on her way home. She does a half day, working in the kitchen at one of the large manor houses in the area. Today, she'd been asked to stay for some extra hours to prepare a meal for the evening." He checked his note-book again. "The house is owned by Sir George Glad-stone. He is recently widowed and has a daughter, Petronella Gladstone. I spoke with Sir George briefly to confirm that Elizabeth Handicott worked for him. She is usually driven back to the village but she asked the driver to drop her off. The field is not far from the village so, after collecting her wild flowers, she'd planned on walking the rest of the way."

Taking a sip of her brandy, Evie then said, "She must have been eager to collect those wild flowers." She supposed it was as good as any reason to walk across a field. After all, she and Tom had stopped by a field for the pure enjoyment of it but also to indulge in a moment alone after the strange day they'd had.

"I believe she is trying to decide which flowers she will use for her wedding bouquet," Henry Evans explained.

"Oh," they all chorused.

Henrietta was the first to explain their surprise. "The vicar read the banns today. There were quite a few and I believe that is where we heard her name."

"I'm surprised you heard it. You talked right throughout the reading of the banns," Sara murmured.

"Well, now we know she lives in the village so Evangeline should have no trouble speaking with her." Henrietta glanced at Henry Evans. "Unless, of course, you object."

Henry Evans smiled and cleared his throat. "Officially, I am inclined to remind Lady Woodridge this is a murder investigation."

"Yes, yes, and the police don't like people poking about but you must admit Evangeline has been quite successful in the past and, I might even go so far as to say, she has been instrumental in solving several cases. Surely you won't turn your nose up at the possibility of her solving the case for you."

Tom laughed. "Henry, in your place, I would merely smile and nod."

As the conversations flowed around her, Evie fixated on the field the vicar had been found in.

Was it the only field with wild flowers near the village? Evie patted her pocket and then looked across the room at a dainty desk sitting in a corner.

Reading her intention, Tom stood up. A brief search

through one of the drawers yielded what she'd wanted—a pen and a notebook.

"Thank you." She wrote the young woman's name. Evie paused and thought how quickly one jumped to conclusions. The banns had been read so she assumed Elizabeth Handicott was young.

Next, she wrote her first question.

Why that particular field?

"Evangeline has hit upon an idea."

"I have, more or less." She lowered her pen and looked at Henry Evans. "Detective —"

"That's a relief. It's been decided," Henrietta whispered. "He is investigating the case, so we will refer to him as detective."

"If you wish to call me Henry, please do. Actually, I would prefer it."

Distracted by Henrietta, Evie forgot what she was going to ask. She searched her mind and just as the question came back to her, the door opened and Edmonds walked in.

"Here's our champion," Henrietta exclaimed. "You have done the House of Woodridge proud."

"After receiving reports of some sort of upheaval in the village," Evie explained, "I asked Edmonds to go out in search of information."

Henry Evans acknowledged Edmonds with a nod.

"Can you tell us what happened, Edmonds?" Evie asked.

"I went to the village first, my lady. There were many stories floating around. I even heard mention of a headless rider. But everyone seemed to be in agreement about the incident being only a mile north of the village."

Evie tried to picture the area. They had actually traveled through it that very day.

"Anyhow, I decided to drive out there and see for myself. It wasn't long before I came up to the scene. I could tell straightaway because there was a police motor stopped by the side of the road."

"Before or after the turn-off?" She remembered seeing the vicar emerging from a side lane not far from the village.

Edmonds nodded. "The police were stationed just before that lane and the constables were standing right in front of it, as if to stop anyone from turning into it. I doubt I would have been able to turn into it. They looked determined to stop anyone from doing so. I stopped and walked along the road to get closer. At one point, I stopped to look across the field."

"If memory serves, there are trees lining that lane." She recalled seeing the vicar's car only as it pulled into the road they were traveling along.

Edmonds confirmed it. "I've driven along it. There's a farmhouse on the left. I believe it's standing vacant."

"And the field is on the right of the lane?" Evie asked.

"Yes."

Evie realized that had been the field she and Tom had stopped at.

"When did the police attack you?" Henrietta asked.

"As I was saying, I was standing there looking across the field. I had to clamber up the rise to get a better look. That's when they tackled me."

"And you fought them off valiantly," Henrietta said.

"I tried to, my lady." Edmonds smiled. "As one of them pulled me back, I was still looking across the field and that's when I saw a man straightening. Another constable. I assume that's where the body was found." Edmonds looked at Henry Evans.

She and Tom had returned late in the afternoon. This must have happened after they'd driven through the area. On their return, they hadn't driven through the village. So they had missed seeing the commotion. If there had been one. She gave a pensive nod of her head. Yes, it must all have happened after they left the field.

Evie shook her head. "What time did Elizabeth Handicott stop to collect the wild flowers?"

"After five," Henry Evans said.

That was well after she and Tom had stopped to rest. Evie opened her notebook and made a note of it. "Tom and I stopped by that field today. We'd been out driving and decided to take a break."

"If memory serves, an hour before," Tom said.

Henry Evans opened his notebook and made a note. "Are you sure you stopped at that particular field?"

Tom nodded. "We were returning to Halton House and stopped just after that lane lined with trees.

Had the vicar already been there? Dead? Or had he been killed after they'd left?

Henry Evans continued writing. "I think this might narrow the timeline."

"Have you found the weapon?" Evie asked.

"The killer used a rock."

"Do you think there was a struggle?"

"No. We believe the vicar was caught by surprise and hit from behind."

Had the vicar been ambushed?

Evie looked at her glass. "It's an open field and it's

mostly covered by tall grass and a profusion of wild flowers. I remember thinking it was fine to walk along because it all came up to our knees. Tom and I walked for a while looking for a clearing." Shaking her head, she added, "I can't see how someone would have caught him by surprise."

"He might have known the person," Tom suggested.

"Yes, but why meet in a field?"

Tom shrugged. "For the same reason we went there?"

A moment to themselves?

Henrietta looked at Evie and then at Tom. "Yes, about that... Why did you go to a field? We have an enormous park here with surrounding woods and I'm sure we have wild flowers."

"We were on our way back from our long drive, Henrietta, and we wanted to stop and stretch our legs." Evie smiled. "It was such a pretty day today, it seemed a shame not to stop and appreciate it."

Henrietta looked at Henry Evans. "I hope that explanation is satisfactory, detective. Evangeline has volunteered the information, so she can't possibly be included in your list of suspects."

Evie and Tom gaped at Henrietta.

6

*H*enry Evans turned to Evie and asked, "What can you tell me about the vicar?"

Henrietta shifted forward. "Is Evangeline being officially questioned?"

"Lady Henrietta, rest assured, Lady Woodridge is not a suspect."

"Why not? After all, by her own admission, she was at the scene of the crime. Also, you are on first name terms yet you just employed a formal address. That tells me you are trying to distance yourself."

"Henrietta," Sara exclaimed. "What are you doing?"

"Sara, isn't it enough to contend with the uncertainty of life? Wherever possible, I wish to seek a firm assurance. I believe the detective can provide it."

Henry Evans hid his smile. "Lady Henrietta, Lady Woodridge... Evie is not a person of interest in this case."

Henrietta raised an eyebrow. "What about Tom? He was with her."

"Mr. Winchester is not a person of interest in this case either."

"Mr. Winchester?"

"Tom," he corrected himself.

Appearing to be satisfied, Henrietta sat back.

As Toodles and Sara looked at her, Henrietta murmured, "He says that now but he might change his mind later on. Evangeline should proceed with caution and take care of how she phrases her responses. She wouldn't want to incriminate herself."

Evie settled back and turned her thoughts to what she knew about the vicar. To her dismay and astonishment, she couldn't think of anything, other than Henrietta's observations made that morning.

The previous vicar's departure had come as a surprise when he'd suddenly announced his upcoming marriage and decision to move to Wales where his future wife hailed from.

His replacement had arrived within twenty-four hours and, shortly after his arrival, the Reverend Jeremiah Stamford had come to Halton House to introduce himself, however, his visit had been brief.

Had he mentioned anything about his past? Evie couldn't remember delving into his life. Then again, her mind had been otherwise engaged.

The dowagers and Toodles had already been advised to take to their beds and stay there until they were fully recovered. With all the cases of Spanish flu he'd had to deal with fresh in his mind, Doctor Weston hadn't wanted to take any risks. In his opinion, their colds had been severe enough to take preventative measures and avoid anything worse, such as pneumonia.

"We first met him during an impromptu visit. Tom and I had just returned from a walk around the park and found the vicar waiting for us in the drawing room." Evie looked at Tom. "I remember being surprised because, as we approached the house, I didn't see any sign of a visitor. Do you remember seeing his motor car?" She certainly didn't.

"Not that I can remember. Isn't that odd."

"I suppose he must have walked from the village. However..." Evie broke off and thought about Mrs. Leeds' remarks that morning.

"However?" Henry Evans prompted her.

"Well, we've since formed a different picture of him. He's been seen zipping about the village in his flashy roadster, I am having difficulty thinking of him as having walked here from the village." Evie shrugged. "That's probably an unfair assumption. At the time of our first meeting I had been greatly preoccupied with other matters. Perhaps I didn't notice his roadster."

Tom shook his head. "It would be difficult to miss, Countess."

She smiled at Tom and knew he understood the meaning of her smile. It always happened when he used her title as a form of endearment.

"Yes, of course. However, I was trying to justify my failure to remember."

"You should contact the bishop," Henrietta suggested.

Henry Evans made a note of it.

"Edmonds. You must remember the first day the vicar came to visit."

Edmonds nodded. "Yes, I do indeed, my lady. The

news spread to the servants' hall within minutes of his arrival."

"Do you know if he drove here?"

"I doubt he did, my lady. Otherwise, someone would have mentioned the motor. Everyone was talking about it in the village today."

"Yes, I heard a story about his driving this morning." At the time, she'd decided she would need to have a word with him and remind him of his duties to his parish.

"He nearly ran Phillipa off the road," Henrietta said.

"Phillipa Brady?" Henry Evans asked.

"Yes, she came for a brief visit today and is now on her way to conquer the new world."

"Phillipa is sailing to New York tomorrow," Sara clarified.

"Marvelous," Henry Evans said and looked down at his notebook.

The clock struck the hour and everyone looked at it with surprise.

"I had no idea it was so late." Henrietta looked at Evie. "All this excitement has worn me out but if you are going to continue discussing the matter, I suppose I can make an effort."

"I wouldn't dream of depriving you of your much-needed rest, Henrietta."

Henry Evans put away his notebook and stood up. "I have an early start tomorrow."

"Edgar will show you to your room." Evie set her glass down. When she stood up, everyone else followed. For a brief moment, she wondered what they would do if she sat down again.

As she thanked Edmonds, Evie saw Henry Evans had

walked on ahead and was out of earshot, so she took the opportunity to ask, "Edmonds, did you notice anyone on your way out to the field?"

"Heading away from it or returning to the village?" he asked.

"Yes, either one." The constables had suspected Edmonds of returning to the scene of the crime. Someone had killed the vicar. Quite possibly, someone who either lived nearby or had lingered just to see what happened next. What if they were hovering near the scene?

"No, but I spent some time in the village and I can't remember ever seeing so many people out and about. Of course, it was a Sunday and quite sunny. I can't help thinking about the constables suspecting me because they thought the killer might return to the scene. Do you think it could be someone from the village?"

"I wouldn't discount the possibility but I don't dare entertain it just yet. Why do you ask?"

He shrugged. "There were a lot of people. Maybe the killer decided to remain in the village to see everyone's reaction. Maybe someone noticed someone acting strangely."

Whenever she saw something odd or out of place, she mulled it over but Tom was always quick to notice and prompt her to share her thoughts. Then, there were the times when she noticed something unusual but she didn't make the connection until later on.

"You think someone in the village knows something they are not sharing?"

"I'm not accusing anyone, my lady. In hindsight, I wish I'd paid closer attention to the people not saying anything. Most of the villagers looked excited to share theories but there were a few who just stood by listening."

"Would you recognize them if you saw them again?"

"I might, but the mind is tricky, my lady."

She couldn't agree more. Everything she'd seen in the village recently could easily become distorted by the thoughts she was entertaining now as well as the events that had taken place.

"Thank you again for doing your very best, Edmonds." She bid him a goodnight and was about to follow the others up the stairs when Tom tugged her back.

"Oh, I thought you'd gone up."

"Nightcap?" he offered.

"I wouldn't mind." Evie joined him by the table, her thoughts in disarray. "I'm hoping everything will make sense tomorrow morning."

"Once we all recover from the shock?"

"Yes." She took the glass he offered and stared at it. "I'm sure there are a set of questions Henry needs answered."

"How, when, and why?" he suggested.

Evie nodded. "And by whom. A man or a woman?"

"He'd only been living in the village for a short while. Is that long enough to make enemies and can we assume it was someone local?"

"If it wasn't someone local, then it would be someone who followed him here and that's why Henry will need to look into his background. Find out where he came from and if he'd had any enemies. I dread to think of the alternative."

"What would that be?"

"A random attack. Someone killing for no good reason."

Tom raised his glass and studied his drink. "Do you think Henry will want us to become involved?"

"He can't expect us to sit back and do nothing. I'm sure he'll understand if we poke around and ask a few questions."

"Where do you propose we start?"

"Mrs. Leeds," Evie suggested. "She seems to know a great deal about the vicar's comings and goings." At any other time, Evie thought, Mrs. Leeds would be perceived as the village gossip and busybody. Now, of course, she would be the font of knowledge.

Tom gave her a brisk smile. "And should we tell Henry of our plans to visit Mrs. Leeds?"

Pondering the question, Evie took a sip of her drink. "He might discourage it and he'd have a right to do so."

"Why?"

"The usual reason. The police don't care for outsiders poking their noses where they shouldn't. However, I'm entertaining another idea. Isn't it strange that we can't remember if he drove here or walked here? I suppose if we start asking questions, we risk seeding false memories. Henry is the detective and he's trained to ask the right questions. I wouldn't want to interfere with his investigation."

"So we're not going to poke around?"

"Thank goodness I've never been presumptuous enough to think I know better. Henry will get to the bottom of this." Evie lifted the glass and smiled. "However... I don't really see any harm in having a chat with

Mrs. Leeds. We could spend some time in the village and try to eavesdrop on conversations. They could be very revealing." She smiled. "Did I just contradict myself?"

"Yes, I think you did." Tom frowned. "It's an odd business."

"It certainly is, but I don't want to think about it too much. Otherwise, I'll never get any sleep."

He lifted an eyebrow.

"Fine, spit it out."

"The timing of events." Tom shrugged. "The vicar seems to have covered a lot of territory."

Yes, indeed. The vicar had been sighted in a couple of places by different people at different times.

Evie nodded. "We should try to put something down on paper. We'll then have something to refer to and it might offer some clarity during those ever so critical moments when we feel we've hit a brick wall."

Tom laughed. "We're usually overwhelmed by too much information or disappointed by the lack of progress."

"Or we're distracted by something else happening around us."

They both sighed.

"Do we start with Sunday service?" Tom asked.

"Yes, of course. He was definitely there. Or was he?"

"What do you mean?"

"He was physically present but his thoughts might have been elsewhere. He might have been thinking about where he needed to be later in the day." Evie thought back to something Henrietta had said. "He spoke to only a few members of the congregation. As in, he addressed everyone but he appeared to only look at a few people.

That could be a trait but we didn't know him long enough to understand his mannerisms." After a moment, she added, "Sometimes, instead of looking at the dowagers and Toodles while I'm talking, I stare into space. Or I fix my gaze on only one of them, even though I'm talking to everyone."

Tom nodded. "We could start by trying to place everyone at the church. Who sat where."

"That could turn into quite an undertaking but it is the best place to start, and then we'll have to work out where the vicar was looking. His focus definitely bounced between only a handful of people." Finishing her drink, she said, "Yes, you're right, the church is a good place to start. I only wish I'd paid more attention to people when we stepped outside. Edmonds had been waiting by the motor. He might have noticed something."

"I suppose it's a case of looking but not seeing."

Evie smiled. "Because you don't know what you're looking for. I'm going to cross my fingers and hope he wakes up tomorrow with a head full of vibrant images." She set her glass down and sighed. "I enjoyed our little escape to the field today. I'd hoped it would save the day. Now it's been ruined."

Moments later, Evie sat at her dressing table with Millicent fussing around the room.

"I heard about the commotion, milady, but I was too preoccupied with Merrin not arriving to find out more."

"We still haven't heard from her? That's worrying

and... heavens, I feel guilty now because I'd almost forgotten about her."

"That's perfectly understandable, milady. Edmonds came down to the servants' hall and told us about his encounter with the constables. In his place, I don't think I would have been so amused."

"No, Millicent. This is not acceptable."

"I'm... Oh, dear. I didn't expect you to react that way. I'm sure Edmonds was quite serious when he investigated on your behalf."

"Who?"

"Edmonds."

"Oh, I was actually thinking about Merrin." Evie sighed. "Earlier this morning, I was caught between Mrs. Leeds and Mrs. Higgins and they were both talking about two different subjects and now my head is still spinning."

Millicent nodded. "Yes, as I said, at least I think I said it, I am greatly concerned about her. Let me think. Yes, I'm sure I mentioned being preoccupied."

"You did, Millicent. We should focus on Merrin. What if something happened to her? I'd never forgive myself."

"Do you think she's missing? I entertained all those dreadful scenarios but then I talked myself out of fixating on all those disturbing thoughts because I really shouldn't be focusing on things I don't wish to happen."

"Do you think she's been happy here?" Evie asked.

"Happy? Who wouldn't be happy working here?"

"Even so, we are rather odd. Perhaps we didn't suit her."

"You? Not suit her? But you're ever so kind, milady."

"It's very generous of you to say so, Millicent, however, I realize I'm not everyone's cup of tea. Also, we do lead different lives to other people. Not every countess goes about looking for killers and thieves... We must remember Merrin had a dreadful experience when she was accused of murder. That short time she spent in jail might have scarred her. I wouldn't blame her if she wanted a more sedate pace and a household that's not constantly in an upheaval."

"What will you do, milady?"

"Detective Inspector Evans is here so I will ask him tomorrow morning. He'll know what to do and whom to contact for more information."

Millicent instantly cheered up. "Is Caro here? I mean, Lady Evans."

"No, he's here as a detective investigating the vicar's death."

"I still can't believe he's dead, milady. You know, I actually missed this morning's service but I attended last week's service and he seemed so nice."

Evie frowned. "Nice? In what way?"

"In a nice way, milady." Millicent shrugged. "Some vicars can sound stuffy and superior. This one sounded approachable."

"Henrietta thinks his voice squeaked. I must admit, I hadn't noticed."

"I'm not surprised. You always have so much on your mind, milady. It's possible his voice squeaked because he was coming down with a cold." Millicent tidied up the dressing table and looked to see if she had set a glass of water for Evie. "Will you and Mr. Winchester be investigating the vicar's death?"

"We shouldn't really. I don't wish to test the detective."

"I would bet anything he'd welcome your input. After all, he came here."

"That's because he couldn't find a room at the pub."

As she finished preparing for bed, Evie changed the subject and told Millicent about Phillipa's visit.

"Don't you wish you could travel with her?" Millicent asked.

"Oh, do you think that's why she came here?"

"In her place, I'd be both excited and worried. Of course, I've never traveled far, whereas she has. Still, I'd need courage to face it all alone."

"She didn't mention anything. However, you're right. I'd love to go along to offer my support. After all, this is her big break. Of course, I'm very happy for her. I want her to do well but, I suppose if I have to be perfectly honest, I fear she might never return."

"I'm sure she will, milady."

"Sometimes, we must accept the fact life will lead us along different paths and those paths will never connect again." Evie surged to her feet. Walking to her bed, she picked up the book she'd been reading. "No, this is too melancholic. I need something cheerful. Doesn't anyone write happy stories?"

"Would you like to borrow my copy of The Wonderful Wizard of Oz?"

Evie thought about falling asleep and dreaming of waking up in a strange land.

"Elizabethan poems?" Millicent suggested and, to Evie's surprise, dug inside her pocket and drew out a small tome.

"You carry this around with you?"

Millicent grinned. "I'm trying to impress Edgar by reciting a poem."

"Wonderful. Which one are you going to recite?"

"I haven't decided yet. First, I need to find one that I can understand." Millicent blushed. "Actually, I need to find one with words I can pronounce easily. I get muddled with all those thine and thou words."

Evie took the book and thanked her. "I'll search for one and you could actually change the words. Make the poem your own."

"You can do that?"

"Of course. Where there are rules, there are also rule breakers."

_____

7

I wonder, by my troth, what thou and I did, till we loved

John Donne

The next morning

*E*vie peeled an eye open and surveyed the room. As she listened, she heard only silence. There were no thoughts hollering for attention and no alarming reminders.

Surprised to find her mind clear of the previous day's woes, Evie yawned and stretched. "Good morning, Millicent."

Millicent barely stopped to murmur a greeting before scurrying about the room to finish selecting the clothes for Evie to wear that morning. "Will you be changing for luncheon, milady?"

Evie smiled and sat up. "If only that could be my only concern for the day."

"I'll bring something out, just in case you decide to change."

Evie searched her mind and remembered she had made plans with Tom. "Mr. Winchester and I are going to the village today. I think I should dress for comfort."

Millicent held out a pair of shoes. "These ones go with the outfit I selected for you."

"Perhaps something with a lower heel, please."

"How much walking do you intend doing?"

"I couldn't really say, Millicent." She pushed herself off the bed and stood up. "Oh, wait. We're only visiting Mrs. Leeds. So we'll be driving right to her house. However, we're bound to wander around the village. Tom expressed an interest in becoming better acquainted with all the gardens. Or was it the streets?"

"And what will Lord Evans think of you calling on Mrs. Leeds?"

Evie thought they would cross that particular bridge when they came to it. "I suppose it depends on what we can come up with. If we have a fruitful morning, he'll be pleased. That presents quite a challenge for us because I have first-hand experience listening to Mrs. Leeds." Forewarned is forearmed, she thought. She already knew Mrs. Leeds enjoyed the sound of her own voice. Asking pointed questions would get them some yes and no answers, but Evie imagined asking loosely phrased questions would give Mrs. Leeds some wiggle room to express herself more freely. That's when they might actually discover something they hadn't even considered.

Evie decided she would take her time preparing for the morning. She wanted answers but she didn't want to leave it to chance. If only she could formulate a plan. "Do you know if Mr. Winchester is downstairs?"

"I believe he is, milady."

Evie wrote a brief note and asked Millicent to take it down to the dining room.

Puzzled, Millicent asked, "Do you expect an answer from him?"

"No, I've just written a note asking him to remind me to talk to Lord Evans about Merrin. Once I go down, I might be sidetracked and I don't wish to end the day without news or taking some sort of action."

Millicent hurried out, leaving Evie to deal with her thoughts. She didn't want to fall into the trap of dreading the worst. If something had happened to Merrin, someone would have contacted them by now.

As she dressed, she focused on the task ahead.

Elizabeth Handicott had found the body.

Evie didn't know where every villager lived so she would have to find someone who did. Then, there was the timing of their visit. She didn't want to go behind Lord Evans' back. Assuming he would speak with Elizabeth Handicott again, she decided to wait and see how he fared. If he didn't get any new information out of Elizabeth Handicott, she might then suggest she and Tom have a word with the young woman. "At which point, we can ask Lord Evans for the address."

By the time Millicent returned, Evie had finished dressing and was fastening the buckles on her shoes.

"Lord Evans and Mr. Winchester are having breakfast, milady. As I stepped out, I heard Mr. Winchester asking Lord Evans how best to search for a missing person."

"Perfect. We'll soon know how to proceed." Evie smiled at Millicent. "Don't worry. We'll have this sorted out soon."

Satisfied with the way she had organized her morning, she inspected her reflection in the mirror, saying, "I wonder, by my troth, what thou and I did, till we loved."

Millicent blinked but didn't say anything.

"It's the first line of a poem by John Donne. It celebrates young love."

"Oh."

"Millicent? You said you wanted to surprise Edgar with a poem."

"Yes. I just didn't think you would do something about it so soon."

"I thought you could work on memorizing that line and then we could work on the rest. It's not very long. Edgar will be impressed."

"Thou," Millicent murmured. "Do you think Edgar would notice if I changed thou to you?"

"I doubt he will, Millicent." Selecting a scent bottle, she dabbed some scent on her wrist. Lord Evans' question about the vicar had made Evie realize she knew next to nothing about him. She'd need to rectify that. "By the way, do you want to see what you can find out about the vicar?"

Millicent brightened. "Oh, yes, please."

Feeling she had geared herself up to start the day on the right footing, Evie made her way down to breakfast.

She entered the dining room and found Tom helping

himself to a cup of coffee.

He was alone.

"Where's Henry?"

"Good morning to you too." Tom took a leisurely sip of his coffee before saying, "Henry wanted to get an early start."

"Oh."

Edgar entered, followed by a footman carrying a tray.

"This arrived for you just now, my lady." He held out a salver with an envelope on it.

Evie thanked him and took the letter. Distracted by Lord Evans' absence, she grumbled, "So much for organizing my morning."

"Poor Henry." Tom laughed. "He's ruined your day and he doesn't even know it."

Helping herself to some eggs and toast, Evie then sat down opposite Tom. "I'd hoped... No, actually, I'd expected to find Henry here. He must know we won't be satisfied with sitting around, twiddling our thumbs while he investigates the vicar's death and leaves us out of the loop."

Tom's eyes glinted. "Yes, it's outrageous."

Evie harrumphed. "I'm glad to provide you with some entertainment, Mr. Winchester."

"Countess, I fail to see what the problem is. Last night, we decided we would speak with Mrs. Leeds today and stay out of Henry's way."

"Yes, but I'd feel more at ease if he knew we were going to spend the morning in the village. Now he'll probably think we're going behind his back." She tore open the envelope only to stop when she was interrupted by another thought. Looking up, she continued, "I also wanted to ask for some advice. Merrin was due to return yesterday. Of course, I realize he's here to investigate a murder and I can't expect him to be at my disposal, but this is turning into an urgent matter. In fact, it is an urgent matter."

Tom's eyebrows hitched up. "You sound frustrated."

"As I said, I was organized."

"Ah, my mistake. You're not frustrated. You're having a tantrum."

Evie laughed. "Yes, I suppose I am. For once, I'd like everything to play out the way I see it unfolding in my mind."

"It must be disappointing to you to realize we are real people, with unpredictable natures. Just as well the dowagers and Toodles have their breakfast in bed. Otherwise, you'd have to contend with whatever surprise they decide to present us with today."

The door to the dining room opened and the dowagers and Toodles walked in.

"I spoke too soon but I believe I just made my point. We are quite unpredictable."

"You don't seem to be," Evie murmured.

Hearing her, Tom smiled. "I aim to be steady and reliable."

Henrietta led the way in, exclaiming, "Oh, wonderful. You are both still here. I was afraid we might have missed a new development."

Tom raised his cup of coffee. "You are just in time to watch us having a leisurely breakfast."

"I don't know about Henrietta and Sara but I intend to do more than watch." Toodles lifted several lids before making her selection for breakfast.

Evie glanced at the letter she held only to look up. "Actually, Henrietta, Tom and I need to engage your assistance. Yours too, Grans and Sara."

"We are going to be accomplices. Marvelous."

"No, Henrietta. Not accomplices. We are not going to commit a crime."

"Partners," Sara suggested.

"I'd bet anything we'll end up being fellow conspirators," Toodles said.

"Will Lord Evans be aware of our activities?" Henrietta asked.

"For now, I think we should keep it to ourselves," Evie suggested.

Henrietta selected a piece of toast and focused on buttering it. "In that case, we will be colluders."

"Very well, if that makes you happy."

"What do you want us to do, Evangeline?"

"We need to draw up a list of people who attended Sunday service. If possible, I'd like to know where each person sat."

Henrietta mused, "I'm not sure I paid enough attention to be of any assistance."

"If you think about it, Henrietta, you'll realize you noticed more than you remember at this moment. For instance, as you entered the church, you cast your eye around. You saw people walking to their seats. You always do. In fact, we all do."

Henrietta brightened. "I see what you mean. Actually, it shouldn't be that difficult because everyone sits in the same places."

"What do you mean?"

"It's simple. The Woodridge family has their pew. We

always sit at the front. Over the years, everyone else has staked a claim on a particular pew." Henrietta smiled. "The Bradford family sit behind us and the Collins family have been trying to edge them out."

"This is news to me. Everyone looks so convivial."

"My dear, Evangeline. You always look for the good in people. In any case, they don't squabble in church, but remarks have been made and they circulate until everyone knows how feelings stand. The Collins family think themselves superior to the Bradford family, who are farmers. The Collins lot arrived in the village twenty years ago and Mr. Collins is a respected solicitor, but the Bradford family have been farming here for over a hundred years. That counts for a lot in these parts." Henrietta lowered her buttering knife and looked up. "Oh, dear. Why was I telling you about all that?"

"Sitting arrangements," Sara prompted.

"Oh, yes. Thank you. We all sit in the same places every Sunday. It's tradition."

Toodles laughed. "The Who's Who of the Village of Woodridge."

"Brilliant. Well done, Henrietta. So, it would be a matter of remembering who was at the service yesterday." The service had been well attended and, if Evie had to guess, she'd say the entire village had been there.

While Evie had been preoccupied with Henrietta's constant chattering, she knew she must have noticed something. In fact, she was convinced that if she took a moment to think about it, she would be surprised by how much she could remember.

Ideally, the exercise should have occurred to her the night before. She often relaxed into a meditative state and that might have helped to create a clear image of what she'd seen as she'd walked in and made her way to the front pew.

Henrietta had made a valid point. Most parishioners enjoyed sitting in the same pews every week. That was definitely a good start.

"May I ask why you want to know this, Evangeline?"

Evie looked at Henrietta. It took her a moment to organize her thoughts. "Yesterday, you made an observation. The vicar focused his attention on only a handful of people. If we can work out where everyone sat, and if we can decide where the vicar was directing his attention, then we might be able to guess who had been the subject of his focus."

"Evangeline, I don't say this often enough, but that is a brilliant idea. Although, I'm not sure why you wish to know that."

Because, Evie thought, someone in the congregation might be responsible for killing the vicar.

"I'm just curious." Evie shrugged and picked up her coffee cup.

"Birdie, are you going to read that letter?" Toodles asked.

Letter?

Evie looked down and realized she was still holding the envelope. Removing the sheet of paper, she read it.

"Oh, dear."

Henrietta leaned in and whispered to Sara, "Is that a good news or bad news *Oh, dear*. I couldn't quite define the intonation."

Evie looked up and said in a flat tone, "It's from Merrin."

8

The village

om maneuvered the motor car around a corner, drove down a narrow street and came to a stop. "Countess? You should talk about it. Keeping it all inside can't possibly do you any good."

Evie noticed he had chosen a strategic spot, diagonally opposite Mrs. Leeds' house, which sat opposite the vicarage.

As they'd driven through the village, she hadn't seen Lord Evans' motor and assumed he had left it in a side street.

"Countess?"

"There's nothing to say. Merrin has chosen to leave Halton House and work elsewhere." Stating her inability to adapt to the unusual rhythm of life at Halton House was something Evie understood perfectly well. Yet it had come as a surprise. What she didn't understand was Merrin's decision to avoid telling her in person. Had she feared being talked out of leaving? Much thought had gone into the decision and Evie had to respect it and accept it.

Dismissing the subject, she said, "Let's hope Mrs. Leeds is home." Climbing out of the roadster, she sighed. In her haste to escape everyone's comments, she had forgotten to tell Millicent the news. Now, she would hear it from someone else. Edgar and a footman had been in the dining room and had heard Toodles and the dowagers expressing several opinions. She didn't think Edgar would bring up the subject but the footman might talk about it in the servants' dining hall.

Shaking her head, she decided the matter would simply have to wait until she returned to Halton House.

"How are we going to explain our visit?" Tom asked.

"Curiosity, of course. Mrs. Leeds mentioned the vicar yesterday so it makes sense for me to see how she feels about the news."

Tom smiled at her. "You don't strike me as the type to go around asking people how they feel about the vicar being killed."

"It will have to do because I can't think of any other excuse."

"Perhaps we should have brought a basket," Tom suggested. "No one expects an explanation for those."

They walked with purpose, crossing the street and following the line of houses until they reached Mrs. Leeds' stone cottage. A profusion of blooms covered the small patch of garden. Evie could see a side gate and imagined a larger garden in the rear of the house.

Tom knocked on the front door and stepped back. "I think I smell scones or maybe it's cake. There's a hint of sugar in the air."

They heard hurried steps approaching, not from within the house, Evie thought, but rather from the rear of the house.

"I'm coming," Mrs. Leeds called out just as she appeared from around the side of the house. "Oh, this is a surprise. Lady Woodridge and Mr. Winchester. I was in the back garden and had the back door opened just so I could hear if someone knocked on the front door. Imagine my surprise when someone did knock. I'm wearing my gardening shoes and they've become muddied so I had to come around the side."

Evie greeted her. "I hope we haven't come at an inconvenient moment, Mrs. Leeds."

Mrs. Leeds looked toward the front door. Evie imagined her debating with herself. After all, she was wearing her gardening shoes. She wouldn't want to enter the house through the front door but she couldn't possibly ask her ladyship to follow her along the path to the rear garden.

Wanting to spare her, Evie said, "It's such a lovely day, Mrs. Leeds. I wonder if it would be too much of an imposition to see your back garden."

"Yes," Tom agreed. "You have a very pretty garden and we were just saying the garden out the back must be even prettier."

"Oh, yes. Of course, do come through."

As if in agreement, Tom and Evie launched a chorus of appreciative remarks about the garden, talking over each other as their eyes feasted on the magnificent display of blooms.

"You have an incredible talent for gardening, Mrs. Leeds." Evie sighed. "It must give you such pleasure, especially at a time such as this one. To think you'd mentioned the vicar only yesterday."

"Such an unexpected tragedy." Mrs. Leeds shook her head. "I rushed over to see Mrs. Higgins as soon as I heard about it. Of course, there was a huge commotion in the village and no one could tell me anything for certain but then the news came and we were all speechless."

Evie had trouble imagining Mrs. Leeds being speechless.

"Soon after you left, I told Mrs. Higgins I would make a point of staying up until the vicar returned as he was bound to go out again and stay out until well after midnight. Several hours later, he was dead. Despite knowing he wouldn't be returning to the vicarage, I sat by the window looking across the street. Force of habit, I suppose."

Evie hurried to slip in a question, "Did he have a housekeeper?"

"Yes, indeed, he did. Mrs. Paterson. She made him breakfast because that was the only meal she knew he would be there to eat. Otherwise, he was always out for lunch and dinner. Now, she'll have to wait and see who the new vicar will be. There's bound to be one soon as there are so many people getting married. Poor Mrs. Paterson. She lives two doors down and feels blessed to only have to cross the street to go to work. The war, you see, left her a widow. Although, even before that, when Mr. Paterson was still around, she used to do the housekeeping for the vicar. He had no business joining up. Mr. Paterson should have known better but he wanted to do his bit for the war effort. He was meant to have a desk job but found himself right in the thick of it..."

Before Mrs. Leeds could continue, Evie hurried to say, "You were at the service yesterday."

Mrs. Leeds nodded.

Evie thought about the task she had given the dowagers and Toodles. If Mrs. Leeds could remember where the parishioners had sat, they could use the information to fill in the gaps. "This might be a strange question. We were discussing it earlier, how people had the habit of sitting in the same pews. Do you?"

"Yes, usually. Although, sometimes, there's someone I meet on my way to church and we end up sitting together. It usually happens when the husband stays home for whatever reason."

"And where did you sit yesterday?"

"I was running late because I'd slept through the alarm. I don't like to set it for Sundays but I'd been having trouble sleeping and thought I might need reminding to wake up. So I set the alarm. A lot of good that did me because I slept right through it. Anyhow, I was running late so I had to sit in one of the back pews. Oh, I suppose I could have found somewhere closer to the front, but I was late. The service had already begun and I didn't want to make a nuisance of myself."

Evie was about to ask if she remembered the people sitting around her when Mrs. Leeds said, "Then I noticed Clara sitting in front of me."

"Mrs. Higgins' niece?"

"That's right. There was an empty space next to her so

I moved up. One doesn't want to seem unfriendly. Although, I wish I hadn't sat next to her because she kept fidgeting. The poor girl seems to have developed a nervous disposition. Then again, I don't blame her. Tessa can be very particular about her food and Clara is not really much of a cook."

"How far back were you sitting?"

Mrs. Leeds looked up in thought. "It might have been the second pew from the back." She nodded. "Yes, and then I moved to the next one to join Clara. She told me she wanted to dash out as soon as the service ended because she needed to make lunch for her aunt."

"Was there any room in the last pew?"

"Not along the aisle. I didn't want to ask people to move or let me through."

Evie looked at Tom who asked, "And on which side of the church did you sit?"

Mrs. Leeds looked surprised at the question. "The left."

"Can you remember who was sitting around you?"

"I'm not sure. I'd been trying to decide what to have for lunch and then Clara was fidgeting. I was also distracted by the scent. That's another reason I moved. If Clara hadn't been sitting in front of me, I still would have moved up."

"Because of the scent?" Evie asked.

"Yes, I didn't want to turn around so I couldn't tell you who it was, but I found the scent not to my liking. I have a sensitive nose, you see. It was lovely but a tad excessive."

"What did it smell like?"

"Jasmine. A whole bottle of it."

Evie thought Mrs. Leeds had to be exaggerating. If the

scent had been that strong, she would have smelled it, either when she'd entered the church or when she's made her way out. Yes, she had been preoccupied but not enough to miss a strong scent.

Evie decided Mrs. Leeds couldn't really help them identify the people the vicar had focused on because she'd been sitting too far back.

While she hadn't noticed his gaze bouncing around, she was sure he hadn't been looking all the way down the back of the church.

"Was it a familiar scent?" Tom asked.

Mrs. Leeds hummed. "No, I don't think so. People generally don't wear heavy scents to church. If they do, it's something familiar like lavender and most likely to be soap."

"And you didn't see the woman."

"I remember thinking I would look at her on my way out but then I forgot. As soon as the service ended, Clara rushed past me and I followed her out. Not necessarily because I was in a hurry. I might have been prompted by Clara's swift exit. Although, I did have a lot to do at home, and people usually shuffle out of church and take their time saying a few words to the vicar. I wanted to avoid that." Mrs. Leeds tilted her head and smiled. "Are you, by any chance, looking into the vicar's death?"

Evie decided to explain, "Someone noticed the vicar had been focusing his attention on a select few parishioners."

Mrs. Leeds proved to be quite astute. "I see, and you think you can identify the persons of interest if you know who sat where."

"Precisely."

Lowering her voice, Mrs. Leeds said, "Was he murdered?"

Of course, Evie only then realized the police hadn't released all the information about the vicar's death. If she answered, she would be responsible for breeching Henry Evans' confidence. Although, strictly speaking, he hadn't asked her to keep the information to herself.

Tom rescued her by saying, "The police will, no doubt, release that information to the public in due course." He then won Evie's gratitude by looking at his watch. "Oh, is that the time?"

"But I haven't even offered you tea. What will everyone say if they know you came by and walked away with nothing?"

"You should say we were only interested in seeing your lovely garden, Mrs. Leeds."

They left the way they came in, with Tom saying, "We forgot to ask where Elizabeth Handicott lives."

How else could they find out her address? "Is it too early for the pub?"

"I believe so."

Exasperated with herself for forgetting, Evie looked up and across the street. "Oh, there's Henry, coming out of the vicarage. We should hurry before he sees us."

"Too late. He's waving."

And walking toward them with purpose. "We'll say we met Mrs. Leeds yesterday and were keen to see her garden because Mrs. Higgins said it was the most beautiful one in the village."

Tom snorted. "And you think Henry will believe you?"

They crossed the street and met Henry Evans, who had brought out his notebook. Turning several pages, he then looked up and shook his head. "You've just been to see Mrs. Leeds."

"Do you have everyone's name and address noted down?" Tom asked.

"Only a few. I'm told I should speak with Mrs. Leeds because she's an interesting character who is well informed."

"Who told you that?" Evie asked.

"Mrs. Paterson, the vicar's housekeeper. I've just been having a chat with her. I wanted to know about the vicar's daily habits and I'm told Mrs. Leeds is probably the only person who can give me an accurate account of his comings and goings."

"Have you spoken with Elizabeth Handicott?" Evie asked.

"Yes, but I'm afraid I didn't get anything worthwhile out of her."

"Do you know if she attended Sunday service?" She had gone in to work for Sir George Gladstone but she might have gone to church first.

"I didn't ask." Henry Evans tipped his hat back and studied Evie.

"Oh, I assumed you wanted to know where everyone was."

"Before the vicar was killed?" Henry Evans crossed his arms. "What am I missing?" His gaze bounced between Evie and Tom.

"My chauffeur, Edmonds, was detained on the suspicion of returning to the scene of the crime. So, Tom and I have been entertaining the idea of the killer attending Sunday service."

"Watching his prey?"

"Yes." Evie saw Lord Evans doing his very best to suppress a smile.

"Henry?" Tom prompted.

Drawing in a deep breath, Henry Evans cast his gaze along the street. "In other words, you both suspect the entire village, because everyone in the village attended Sunday service."

"I wouldn't quite put it like that," Evie objected. "Mrs. Leeds attended the service and I'm sure she didn't kill the vicar."

Henry Evans raised an eyebrow. "Why?"

Oh, dear. Why indeed. Did she drive? Evie didn't think so. "How would she get to the field? On foot?" It only took five minutes to reach the field by motor car, at least at the speed Tom drove, but it would take a lot longer on foot.

Evie shook her head. "She had lunch with Mrs. Higgins."

"Are you sure about that?" he asked.

Evie nodded. Although, in reality, she knew her assumption was based on the fact Mrs. Higgins' niece had been cooking and Mrs. Leeds had arrived just before lunch.

"That's three names off your list of suspects. Clara Dalgety is visiting and she was at Mrs. Higgins' house preparing lunch. I assume the vicar was killed sometime during the middle of the afternoon but Clara Dalgety is here to look after her aunt. She would not have left her alone."

Henry Evans hitched his head slightly, prompting Evie to turn.

Mrs. Leeds was hurrying down the street toward a

motor car. She climbed in and the motor promptly disappeared around the corner.

"Well... She was a passenger and not the driver. Actually... How on earth did she manage to leave so quickly? We just spoke with her a few minutes ago and she'd been busy gardening."

Tom looked at his watch. "Fifteen minutes, to be precise."

"That still doesn't explain how she could have hurried out so quickly. Tom, did you see the motor car?"

He nodded. "I believe it was an Austin."

"Would you recognize it if you saw it again?" Evie asked.

Both Tom and Henry Evans turned toward the street that cut through the village. They didn't have long to wait before a motor car appeared.

It was the same motor car. "Different color," Evie murmured. "I suppose they're quite affordable cars."

"Yes, but the question remains," Tom said, "how did Mrs. Leeds manage to leave the house so quickly?"

Lord Evans looked at his watch. "I should get on with it. I still have several people to see this morning."

"Can we expect you for lunch?" Evie asked.

"I couldn't promise it so it might be best if I stop by the pub." He thanked her and turned away to leave only to stop. "By the way, I went through the vicar's appointment book. It seems you were both going to see him later in the week. Were you seeking spiritual guidance?"

Evie gave him a brisk smile. "Always." She gave Tom's sleeve a tug.

"Oh, yes. We must get going or we'll be late." As they

walked away, he murmured, "Why are we being secretive?"

"Because the vicar's death might delay our plans and we don't wish to get everyone excited for no good reason."

"No, we wouldn't want that."

When they reached the corner, Evie looked over her shoulder. "Come on. Henry's out of sight."

"Where are we going?"

"To speak with the vicar's housekeeper, of course. What was her name?"

"Mrs. Paterson. Why do we want to speak with her?"

"She might tell us what they talked about."

Tom looked heavenward. "If Henry had learned anything significant, he would have shared it with us."

Evie laughed. "You put a lot of trust in your male camaraderie."

They hurried along the path leading to the vicarage and saw the housekeeper busy cleaning the windows from the inside.

Approaching the front door, Evie mused, "After this, we might visit Mrs. Higgins again."

"Why? She didn't attend the service."

"No, she didn't, but she'll be able to tell us if Mrs. Leeds stayed for lunch. Otherwise, we'll have to either rely on Henry to tell us or have another chat with Mrs. Leeds."

"Yes, I see. We'd have to come up with another reason for visiting her. She already suspects we're looking into the vicar's death."

"That's right. We wouldn't want her to think we suspect her."

"Do we?" Tom asked.

"Not really. I can't imagine Mrs. Leeds asking someone to drive her to the field so she could meet the vicar and kill him." Evie stopped. "Meet the vicar." She looked at Tom.

"What?"

"Have we asked ourselves what he was doing in the field?"

"I suppose we must assume he was there to meet someone."

"A secret assignation?"

"He was a busy man. Where did he go every day? And whom did he meet?"

Evie nodded. "Something or someone kept him out until late."

"Let's hope Henry gets to the truth soon. Otherwise, the entire village will come to realize you hold them under suspicion." Tom knocked on the door.

While Evie hadn't known Mrs. Paterson was the vicar's housekeeper, she was acquainted with Mrs. Paterson but she couldn't remember ever talking with her.

When the door opened, the middle-aged Mrs. Paterson smiled. "Your ladyship, I thought I saw you talking to that lovely detective. My eyesight is not what it used to be so I wasn't really sure."

"Mrs. Paterson, I wonder if we could steal a moment of your valuable time."

She waved them in, saying, "Dreadful news about the vicar. So young. His family will be devastated."

"Do you know if they have made arrangements?"

Mrs. Paterson nodded. "I've been asked by those

higher up to get the vicarage ready. The service will be held here, which is rather odd."

"Why is that?"

"His family is from Norwich and well-to-do." Mrs. Paterson showed them through to the drawing room and offered them tea.

"Thank you, but we won't be staying long."

"I suppose you want to know if I suspect someone," Mrs. Paterson offered.

"Is that what the detective asked you?"

"He didn't come straight out with it. In fact, I've taken the liberty to jump to conclusions." Mrs. Paterson smiled and tapped her nose. "He wanted to know if there had been any disagreements with anyone. Of course, I couldn't really answer that question because the vicar was rarely here."

"Yes, about that... Do you have any idea where he went?"

"None whatsoever but he was always happy to be dashing off. As if he looked forward to it."

"And he never mentioned any names?"

Mrs. Paterson shook her head. "I was curious but I could never figure out a way to ask him without it sounding out of place."

He'd only been in the village for three weeks. "These outings of his, when did they start?"

"Let me think. The first day, he actually told me he was going out exploring the village and the countryside. I assumed he wanted to become acquainted with the village and the surrounding area. It's all very pretty at this time of the year. He was gone for most of the day and returned late that night. Over the following days, he began to stay out even later. I live across the street, so I always heard that motor of his rambling up the street."

Evie prodded her mind, looking for something relevant to ask. She was about to abandon the effort when she thought of one other person they might speak to. "The verger." She looked around the drawing room, almost as if she expected him to suddenly materialize. In fact, she was trying to remember the man's name.

Rodney?

Rodney... Hale.

She turned her attention back to Mrs. Paterson only to find her shaking her head.

"The vicar didn't take to him."

"What?" Evie had never heard anything so preposterous. The very idea of not liking someone whose priority was to assist them in their duties simply didn't register in her mind.

Evie couldn't imagine arriving at Halton House as the new chatelaine and not taking to Edgar or Mrs. Arnold, the housekeeper, or the cook, Mrs. Horace. She thought of every servant at Halton House and couldn't imagine questioning their presence there. If their personalities clashed, then it was her duty to establish some sort of working relationship.

"He simply didn't care for him. He won't do, that's what he said. Poor Rodney, he was devastated. This was his entire life." Mrs. Paterson lowered her voice. "He hasn't been himself since he came back."

Evie didn't need Mrs. Paterson to explain.

He had served in the trenches.

"His role as verger here gave him a reason to get up every day. Now he rarely leaves his house."

"Where does he live?" Tom asked.

Mrs. Paterson wrote down the address. "He won't know anything."

"Did the vicar get a new verger?"

"No, he did everything himself. Said that's the way he liked it."

How very odd.

"I wish I could help you with more, but that's all I know. I'm sure there are plenty of people wondering what he got up to."

Evie wondered how many people they would have to speak with before finding someone who'd actually seen the vicar out and about on the roads.

They had come across him when they'd headed out to Althea Rawlinson's farm. Suddenly, she remembered Phillipa's encounter with him. Of course, they had no way of confirming it had been the vicar.

Phillipa had been coming from the opposite direction. That meant the vicar had covered a great deal of ground in a single day.

Where had he been headed?

9

Sleuthing under cover

The vicarage

*E*vie and Tom stopped outside the vicarage and looked up and down the street. If they'd remained silent, Evie would have guessed they were both entertaining the same thoughts. But she had to ask...

"What do you make of that?" Evie asked.

"About the vicar getting rid of the verger? Since I don't know Rodney Hale, I couldn't even hazard a guess."

"You don't know him but you've seen him at Sunday service."

"Yes, but I never engaged him in conversation. From a distance, he looked efficient and focused on his job. I suppose that's not the right description of him. Devoted. Yes, he looked devoted."

"What else would we need to know about him?" Evie thought Rodney Hale's behavior reflected much of his character. A quiet man with a devotion to duty. Who could fault that? "It's not as if the vicar replaced him with someone else. I find that curious. Do you think he had a reason for dismissing Rodney Hale?"

"I'm sure he did. It's possible he didn't require any assistance."

"I suppose that might be the case, but I'm not buying it."

"And now you'd like to speak with Rodney Hale."

"I would, but I'd prefer to wait and see if Henry speaks with him."

"You're still intent on staying out of the investigation."

"I'd prefer to be several steps behind Henry. I don't want to be known as the snoopy countess."

"Does your caution have anything to do with Henry warning Caro away from crime detecting?"

Evie nibbled the edge of her lip. "Perhaps... a little. A part of me feels the need to prove myself to him, but I'd like to do that with discretion."

"You won't hear any objections from me. I'm sure you know best." Tom nodded. "Where are we going now?"

Evie gave it some thought. If they remained in the village, they were bound to encounter Lord Evans again. "I'm reluctant to tread on his toes."

"He'll be disappointed if you don't. I doubt he considered the possibility of the killer attending Sunday service. I wouldn't be surprised if he hasn't already altered his entire strategy based solely on your observation."

"I hope that's the case and not necessarily because I influenced him but rather because he might actually identify the killer and we can all get on with our lives."

"That reminds me, are we keeping our appointment this afternoon?"

Evie gasped. "Heavens, I'd almost forgotten about that. Althea will be expecting us." Evie suggested returning to Halton House for luncheon and only then deciding if they should proceed with their planned visit to Althea.

Of course, she couldn't anticipate the unexpected. Anything could happen between now and the afternoon. "With any luck, Millicent will have dug up something interesting about the vicar. She can be rather resourceful and she was almost joyful to be given the task."

Tom smiled. "Yes, being a lady's maid can't be much of a challenge."

"She's my secretary," Evie reminded him.

"That's what I meant to say. She's already had a taste of a higher calling. I doubt she'll want to step down now. I hear her typing is coming along nicely."

"Laugh if you will, Mr. Winchester. I would never dream of stopping Millicent from climbing her ladder. Although, I must admit, I would probably do everything in my power to stop her leaving me."

"If Millicent leaves, Edgar will too. Have you thought about that?"

"Tom, you'll give me nightmares." She looked up and down the street. "Now that I think about it, I'm eager to return to Halton House. Thanks to Mrs. Paterson, we now know the vicar hailed from Norwich."

"And you think Millicent can tap into her web of contacts stretching all the way to Norwich?"

Evie lifted her chin. "I wouldn't dream of underestimating or questioning Millicent's abilities or methods."

"What about Mrs. Higgins?" Tom asked. "You mentioned going to visit her again."

She'd forgotten about that. "Yes, of course. Let's head over to her house now and, hopefully, by the time we arrive we will have come up with a sound excuse for visiting her again."

"She might appreciate the truth," Tom suggested.

"And what truth might that be?"

He gave it some thought. "You make a valid point. I doubt she'll take kindly to you suspecting her or her niece."

"Did I say I suspected them?"

"Perhaps not, but you do want them to provide reasonable alibis. Just to be on the safe side."

And if they couldn't provide proof of their innocence?

What reason would they have for killing the vicar?

Evie didn't for a moment believe one of the villagers was responsible for killing the vicar. He hadn't been here long enough to give anyone a reason.

Then again...

Henrietta had met him for the first time only the day before and she had already formed opinions about him.

"Actually, you're right."

"I am?"

"Yes, we should be honest with Mrs. Higgins. I think she'll enjoy it if we say she might be rather helpful because she is so well informed about everyone's comings and goings." Evie hesitated. "Oh, wait. We could also mention Mrs. Leeds. She's definitely knowledgeable and quite generous with her opinions."

Tom nodded. "Yes, you could say she might know something relevant to the investigation and doesn't even realize it."

Evie looked at her watch. "Clara Dalgety should be banging the pots. I think that's how Mrs. Higgins described her niece's efforts in the kitchen. Anyhow, it will be better to speak to Mrs. Higgins first. That way we can focus on her alone without being distracted."

"But you'll also want to speak with Clara?"

"Yes, I'd like to know why she was fidgeting so much during Sunday service. Did she strike you as the nervous type?"

Tom slowed down his steps. "She was definitely distracted. That could be a natural trait."

Yes, but what had Clara Dalgety been thinking about?

Of course, she'd be the first to admit to entertaining reservations about questioning Mrs. Higgins. Deep down, she couldn't bring herself to seriously consider anyone from the village as a suspect. In reality, she accepted the fact one never really knew a person until they showed their true colors.

She knew the police would be looking for motive and opportunity. Since she was not a member of the police force, she had the freedom to entertain other possibilities and remain open to ideas that might be regarded as inconceivable by the police.

They came up to the house and saw Mrs. Higgins' cat sitting by the front door.

"Do you think she'll let us through?" Tom asked. "She looks like she means business."

He wasn't wrong. Missy Higgins lowered her head and hissed at them.

"We should have brought Holmes with us," Evie murmured.

"Divide and conquer?" Tom suggested. "We split up and go around her."

"Really? I thought you were about to offer yourself as a sacrifice." Evie squared her shoulders and walked along the path, her steps confident and quite determined. She only faltered once when she saw Missy Higgins had no intention of moving. At the last minute, Evie swerved around her, performing a quick step to reach safety.

"The little rascal didn't even blink," Tom grumbled as he hurried along the path, doing his best to duplicate Evie's tactics.

Missy Higgins rolled onto her back, flicked her tail, and yawned.

"She's all hiss and no bite. Or should that be scratch?" Shaking her head, Evie knocked on the door.

"The door is open," Mrs. Higgins called out.

They entered and went through to the drawing room where they found Mrs. Higgins sitting by the window, her leg up on a footstool.

"I asked Clara to keep the door closed. Missy Higgins has spent the morning bringing in a variety of unwanted gifts, including a poor grasshopper. I told her she can come inside through the window but I'll be here to make sure she doesn't bring in any surprises."

"We hope you're feeling better," Evie said.

"Yes, I've been hobbling about today." She looked toward the hallway and lowered her voice, "I'm eager to resume preparing my own meals."

She invited them to sit. Evie chose a chair by the window and Tom stood nearby.

Mrs. Higgins lowered her voice to a whisper, "I suppose you know all about the vicar."

Evie nodded.

"Dreadful, simply dreadful. I hear there's a detective going around asking questions. What do you suppose he thinks we know?"

By 'we' Evie guessed Mrs. Higgins meant the villagers. "Mr. Winchester and I have been asking the same question. Perhaps he thinks someone noticed something or saw a stranger in the village."

"He hasn't come to speak with me. I have been looking out of this window for several days now and I haven't seen anyone suspicious. Thelma Leeds has the best vantage point, living across the vicarage as she does. She also has a view of the main road. She hasn't been by to visit today so I couldn't say if the detective has spoken with her."

"He hasn't. We actually saw her driving away. Or, rather, being driven away."

Mrs. Higgins nodded and didn't seem surprised by the news. "That would be Mr. Howard. They've been driving out to a farm to collect the last of the strawberries and plums. Thelma enjoys making jam. As soon as she finishes making one batch, she starts fretting and thinking it won't be enough to see her through the winter. So off she goes to get more fruit."

So they'd been wrong to be suspicious of Mrs. Leeds' swift exodus. "Has she been driving out every day with Mr. Howard?"

Mrs. Higgins smiled. "Mr. Howard doesn't do

anything on a schedule. Today's trip would have been on a whim. Quite spontaneous."

"I see. And how do they organize it all?"

"He's her neighbor. His house backs onto hers so he only needs to holler over the hedge."

A short while before they had been intrigued to see Mrs. Leeds driving off with great haste and had been quick to jump to conclusions. Now they had no reason to think she was in any way involved in something underhanded.

Admittedly, Evie hadn't known what to make of it all, but at the time, Mrs. Leeds' hurried exit from her house had struck her as odd. Eventually, Evie knew, she would have engaged her imagination and entertained a few possibilities.

Evie glanced around the tidy drawing room and saw a blanket and pillow stacked on the end of a sofa—something she hadn't noticed the day before.

Mrs. Higgins had been sleeping in the drawing room. She supposed this had to do with her inability to move around with ease.

"I must say, you are very lucky to have your niece helping you, Mrs. Higgins. I take it she is here all day."

"Oh, yes. She almost didn't attend Sunday service but I convinced her to go. I feel guilty having her do everything, but she insists. Mr. Wilkes has been delivering the groceries so that's one less task for Clara."

Did that put Clara Dalgety in the clear? Could she have stepped out unnoticed during the afternoon? Evie cleared her throat and dismissed the idea as nonsensical. She might have found the opportunity to sneak out of the house, but what possible reason would she have to kill the vicar?

"She takes her responsibility seriously," Evie mused.

"She's doing her best. Poor dear." Mrs. Higgins lowered her voice. "She's rather keen on a local farmer, but I doubt she has what it takes to be a farmer's wife. She would be required to do everything in the house. There is simply no possibility of ever being able to hide her deficiencies. I blame my sister, of course. I don't mean to be mean spirited and speak ill of her, especially as she can't defend herself... Oh, I do miss her. She married well and had a cook and a local girl doing the housework. So my nieces never had to learn how to keep a home."

"I'm sure she's doing the best she can. As the saying goes, where there is a will, there is always a way." Evie suddenly saw the opportunity to have one of her questions answered without really appearing to ask it. "What did Mrs. Leeds think of yesterday's lunch?"

Mrs. Higgins laughed. "Thelma loves to bake but has no patience with cooking so she always enjoys everything she doesn't have to cook herself. She returned later in the day with a batch of her scones, which was a relief as Clara had been hinting at wanting to try her hand at baking some. I hope to recover before she has the chance. Anyhow, Thelma had been about to have afternoon tea when the commotion erupted. She couldn't find out anything so she came by to wait with me. We thought news would eventually reach us."

Mrs. Higgins looked out the window and waved.

Following her gaze, Evie saw a young woman walking down the path.

"That's Elizabeth Handicott. She came by to teach

Clara how to prepare a dish. She must have left by the kitchen door."

Evie waited to see if Mrs. Higgins mentioned anything about Elizabeth Handicott finding the vicar.

"She's getting married soon." Mrs. Higgins pointed to a motor car. "That's Peter McGraw, her intended. For a moment, I thought it might have been my niece, Margaret. She drives the same motor car."

Evie had to lean slightly forward to see the motor car. It looked quite familiar. In fact, it was the same motor Mr. Howard drove. It took her a moment to remember the model. An Austin in a light shade of gray.

"I assume she doesn't live in the village." Evie wanted to avoid asking a direct question that might lead Mrs. Higgins to question her interest.

"On the outskirts. It's very good of Peter McCraw to drive her in."

At the sound of hurried steps approaching, Evie turned and saw Clara Dalgety coming to a stop at the door to the drawing room.

Seeing her, Clara bobbed a curtsey, something entirely unnecessary, and retreated.

As Mrs. Higgins hadn't mentioned anything about Elizabeth Handicott finding the vicar's body, Evie assumed she didn't know. However, she would soon find out as Evie suspected her niece had just heard all about it and wished to inform her aunt of the latest news.

Evie stood up. "I'm glad to hear you are feeling better, Mrs. Higgins. It must be a great comfort to know you have a relative looking after you. If there is anything we can do for you, do please let us know."

Evie walked out thinking their visit had not been a

complete waste of time as they had succeeded in creating a clearer picture.

They'd already known Mrs. Higgins was housebound, but they now also knew her niece had only stepped out to attend Sunday service. Evie had no reason to doubt Mrs. Higgins. Even her niece's nervous disposition had been explained.

Tom waited until they reached the roadster to say, "Poor Mrs. Higgins will have to endure an overcooked pudding."

"What do you mean?"

"I was being polite. Clara Dalgety burned the pudding. Didn't you smell it?"

"No, I missed it."

"You'll have to do better, Countess."

Evie rolled her eyes. "You're right, of course. Then again, I have you. Did you notice the bedding on the sofa?"

"No, I didn't. But I'm happy for Mrs. Higgins. She has no idea how close she came to being a suspect."

"Well, I hope Henry is having better luck." She looked at her watch. "I suppose we should return. I'm actually eager to see if the dowagers and Toodles managed to get anywhere with the task I set them."

He started the roadster and looked at her. "I'm surprised you haven't brought up the subject of Elizabeth Handicott."

Evie shrugged. "I'm happy to see her out and about. Finding the vicar must have been a dreadful shock."

"Yes, I'm also happy but I can't help finding it odd. She didn't look downcast."

"Not everyone wears their heart on their sleeves. I actually commend her for just getting on with it."

Taking that as a hint, he asked, "Where to now?"

"Let's have a walk around the village. It might clear our heads."

They climbed out of the roadster and headed toward the main street. It looked like any ordinary day, with people going about their business, almost as if nothing had happened.

"Is it possible people have lost interest so soon?" Tom asked.

The footman, Anthony, and Edmonds had seen the village alive with intrigue. According to them, everyone had been out on the street, searching for information.

Evie signaled to a store, which carried all sorts of merchandize. "Let's go in and have a look around. There's bound to be someone in there talking. The owner, Mr. Brown, is an amiable fellow, always eager to have a chat."

"Are we looking for anything in particular?" Tom asked.

"What do you mean?"

"The Countess of Woodridge doesn't usually come in. She sends her lady's maid."

"Why are you referring to me in the third person?"

"Never mind. You look at the haberdashery stock and I'll search for a hammer or a spanner. Yes, a spanner is always useful."

"Don't you have one?"

"I do, but Mr. Brown won't know that."

"I'm sure he'll assume you already have one."

"Evie, my dear, at this point, I can't tell if you are poking fun at me or being sincere."

Evie grinned. "It's called turning the tables. You, Mr. Winchester, always have fun at my expense. I just happen to catch you with your guard down."

They entered the store and were greeted with curiosity.

"I told you," Tom murmured.

They saw a local villager paying for a purchase. Seeing them, the man lingered for a moment and then left.

"This requires a change of tactics." Looking up, Evie smiled at Mr. Brown. His store faced the main street that cut through the village. He would have seen everyone out and about.

Or so she assumed...

A short while later, Tom and Evie stood outside the store.

"What do you make of that?" Tom asked.

"I can't for a moment believe Mr. Brown didn't see or hear anything. Surely someone alerted him to the fact news about something strange happening was spreading throughout the village."

"If he says he was busy stocking the shelves, then we must take him at his word."

"Try saying that with more conviction. He is clearly not telling us the whole truth. Yes, I believe he was stocking his shelves but he must have stopped to look out the window and then he must have stepped out of the store. Or someone came in to discuss the news."

"So you believe he is withholding information."

Evie nodded. "Why would he do that? And don't, for goodness' sake, say because I'm the Countess of

Woodridge and he didn't want to come across as a regular gossip."

"No, I wouldn't say that. But everyone knows you dabble in investigations. I bet anything he was afraid of saying something that might incriminate him."

"Are you suggesting there might be some sort of conspiracy?" Evie looked up and down the street. "That means we are being left out of the loop. When did the villagers lose their confidence in us?"

"Probably when everyone saw us colluding with the police."

"Colluding? Henry Evans is our friend."

Tom laughed. "That's even worse."

10

Disagreements and startling revelations

Halton House

*E*vie and Tom returned to Halton House harboring no great expectations, something Evie thought might actually work in their favor.

The less they thought about something the more likely it was to inspire them with a bright idea. They'd absorbed as much as they could and if anything had fallen between the cracks, it would eventually surface, providing them with an *aha!* moment.

In any case, their morning had failed to yield anything other than what they'd expected to learn.

They had no reason to suspect Mrs. Higgins or her niece. Or even Mrs. Leeds.

Thinking about Mrs. Higgins, Evie wondered what she would say to Mrs. Leeds. Would she mention their visit? If Mrs. Leeds found it odd that they should have returned so soon, she might ponder the reasons why and that might lead her to suspect them of being suspicious of Mrs. Higgins.

Heavens. What would Mrs. Higgins say about that?

Her ladyship suspects me of killing the vicar?

"It might be best to leave the investigation in Henry's capable hands," she mused. "I really don't wish to antagonize anyone."

"There's no harm in working from a distance," Tom suggested. "Henry appears to be willing to accept your ideas."

They walked in and saw Edgar hurrying toward them. Taking Evie's coat, he didn't wait to be asked where the dowagers and Toodles were. "You will find everyone in the dining room, my lady."

Evie looked at her watch. "That's the last place I'd expect them to be at this time of the day. Has luncheon already been served?"

"No, my lady. We've tried to..." Edgar cleared his throat. "That is to say... Well... As a matter of fact..."

"Edgar?" Evie prompted.

"Perhaps you should see for yourself, my lady."

Evie didn't understand Edgar's hesitation. He usually employed a direct, succinct manner, something Evie appreciated, even when she sensed an underlying hint of dry humor.

"Come along, Countess. There's only one way to find out what they're doing."

Evie didn't question Tom's assumption because it was quite obvious the dowagers and Toodles were up to something.

They walked toward the dining room with purpose only to hesitate at the door.

"On the count of three?" Tom suggested.

Evie sighed with resignation and nodded.

As they walked in, they heard Henrietta say, "It's just as I suspected. We have two Mrs. Maisons. That's definitely one Mrs. Maison too many. Sara, pay attention. You need to take better care."

"I am taking great care to write the names on the place cards in a legible hand instead of my usual scrawl. It's not my fault if you have been repeating names."

"I'm thinking out loud. There is a difference."

"In that case, you should state a clear intention."

"And what do you suggest I say?"

"You explain yourself by saying something along the lines of *No need to write that name, Sara. I'm merely expressing my muddled thoughts out loud.*"

Toodles shrugged. "That makes perfect sense to me."

They kept up an amiable running argument, interrupted only when Toodles noticed Tom and Evie.

Hushing Henrietta and Sara, Toodles spread her arms out. "Ta-da. Just as requested."

Evie walked up to the dining table and studied the place cards organized in two sections of rows. She assumed each one represented one row of church pews.

She instantly understood Edgar's dilemma. The place

cards were arranged on the table where they would be sitting down to luncheon.

"In case you are curious, we employed a great deal of reasoning," Henrietta explained. "As everyone has the habit of sitting in the same spot every Sunday, we decided to begin with that and proceeded by trying to remember the people we saw and could place with absolute certainty. Although, we seem to be in disagreement over Mrs. Leeds. I'm beginning to think she wasn't even there, which is strange because I remember noticing her flowers. She always provides flowers for the church. Something else I find strange because in my time the flowers were provided by Halton House. Have we fallen out of favor?"

"Henrietta, you've meandered away from the main subject." Sara stepped forward. "The disagreement stems from other factors. For starters, Henrietta kept referring to Mrs. Leeds as Mrs. Seeds. She thinks my letter L looks like an S."

"That's not what the disagreement was about, Sara. It doesn't help to find people who should be there but aren't."

"Actually, we might be able to help with that." Evie searched for the place card for Mrs. Leeds and found it on the third row. "We spoke with her this morning. She arrived late for the service and sat in the back pew, next to Clara Dalgety." Evie searched for Clara's card but didn't find it.

Henrietta yelped. "Who is Clara Dalgety?"

Evie explained, "She's Mrs. Higgins' niece."

"Does she live in the village? I've never heard of her."

Understanding the confusion, Evie explained, "She's visiting."

"So she doesn't attend the church service on a regular basis but she was there yesterday. How many other people were there that we don't know about?"

That, Evie thought, was a very good question.

"Actually, that brings us to our next disagreement," Henrietta declared. "If Toodles and Sara are to be believed, our vicar was cross-eyed."

Sara shook her head. "I remember him looking toward the pews on the left more than the pews on the right. And, at one point, I'm sure he looked straight down the middle and even squinted, as if he'd been trying to focus his gaze."

Evie looked at the spot where the back pew should have been. "Is there a row missing?"

They all nodded.

"We simply couldn't remember seeing anyone sitting there and yet," Henrietta's shoulders rose and fell, "we know there must have been people because, as Sara insists, the vicar seemed to fixate on that spot."

Evie told them about the scent that had driven Mrs. Leeds to move from one pew to another.

"No, I don't recall a scent," Henrietta said.

Tom stepped forward. "Can we assume it was a woman wearing the scent?"

"Yes, I can't imagine a man wearing a jasmine scent." The person, Evie thought, must have been sitting right on the aisle. Otherwise, Mrs. Leeds could have seen her out of the corner of her eye. Yes, she must have sat directly behind Mrs. Leeds. Would that put the mystery person in sight of the vicar?

Also, had she been a late arrival or had she deliberately sat at the back?

Anyone sitting at the back could have made a discreet exit as soon as the service ended. Indeed, that had been Clara Dalgety's plan as she'd needed to return to her aunt's house quickly so she could prepare lunch.

"What?" Tom asked. "What are you thinking?"

"If this mystery person wanted to go unnoticed, why wear a distinct scent?"

"Perhaps the scent is actually a disguise or a diversion." Tom shrugged. "She might have wanted to conceal the usual scent she wears."

Studying the cards, Evie saw one with a question mark.

Henrietta nudged Sara. "She's noticed it."

"Yes, I have. Why the question mark?"

"After some deliberation, we all agreed we noticed someone sitting at the rear of the church, near the pillar." Henrietta stepped forward and moved the card to the bottom row.

Toodles tapped her finger on the card. "We were walking in when my gaze drifted to the left but, just then, Henrietta shivered."

"I couldn't help it. I always forget the temperature inside the church is always several degrees lower."

Evie tried to remember the moment they'd made their way in. The dowagers and Toodles had arrived first and had already been seated. Her mind had been clear of any concerns, but she must have been thinking about something. Why hadn't she noticed who was sitting where?

"Oh." Cringing, she remembered her thoughts had actually been engaged on their secret assignation.

"What?" Tom asked.

Glancing at him, she rolled her eyes. "I just remembered why I wasn't focusing when we arrived at the church."

"What were you thinking about?" Henrietta asked.

Nibbling the edge of her lip, Evie scrambled to provide an explanation that wouldn't give away what she and Tom had been doing behind their backs.

She had been thinking about their visit to Althea Rawlinson and their meeting with Señor Lopes—something she didn't wish to reveal, just yet.

In an effort to distract them, she asked, "Can any of you remember any details about that person who sat near the pillar? Was it a man or a woman?"

Toodles and Sara chorused, "A man."

While Henrietta chirped, "A woman."

Everyone turned to Henrietta. She shrugged, "Perhaps it was a man. Oh, she or he had very dark hair. Yes, I remember noticing the hair falling over her eyes... or his eyes. Or was it just the one eye?"

Evie looked at Tom in time to see him raise an eyebrow.

Señor Lopes?

Giving the table a sweeping glance, Evie said, "You have all done splendidly. But why did you choose to work here? Why not the library?"

Henrietta harrumphed. "We were banned from the library."

Evie could only think of one person who would have the audacity to declare the library out of bounds.

Millicent.

Henrietta explained, "Your secretary said she needed to focus. I suppose she meant to suggest we would disrupt her but I fail to see how."

Looking up, Evie saw a footman peering in. She didn't need to turn to know Edgar was standing at the other door.

"I think it might be easier if we all work from the same room. We'll have to take these place cards to the library." Evie began collecting them and stopped when Henrietta gasped.

"But they're in order."

"I'll make sure to keep them that way, Henrietta."

"Let's all take a couple of rows," Sara suggested.

Evie and Tom led the way to the library, leaving Edgar to direct the footmen to lay the table for luncheon.

Their steps echoed in the hall. Looking up, Evie imagined the house absorbing the scene, watching their progress and quite possibly being bemused by the antics of the current occupants.

Yes, if only these walls could talk.

Entering the library, they found Millicent holding a focused and intense conversation with herself.

"I'm reluctant to interrupt," Tom murmured.

"Quick, clear your throat."

"On cue?"

"Oh, good heavens. I'll do it." Evie coughed and patted her chest for effect.

"Milady!" Millicent surged to her feet and walked around the desk. "You'll never guess what I discovered about the vicar."

"Heavens!" Evie stopped and stared at the table she

had wanted to use to set up the place cards. "What on earth has happened to the table."

Before Millicent could explain, two footmen entered and tipped soil directly onto the table. Millicent had taken the precaution of laying down several layers of newspaper. Regardless, this looked very odd.

Millicent hurried to the table. Looking very pleased with herself, she explained, "I thought we should have a model of the village and the surrounding area where the vicar was found. We're about to start modeling it."

One of the footmen set a bucket filled with twigs and leaves down on the floor next to the table.

"Those are going to be trees and we'll use gravel for the roads, although, at this scale the gravel will look like boulders. I think sand would be preferable. I thought it might be useful to have a visual aid. From what I've been able to gather, the vicar was found on a field but I've been told Miss Phillipa Brady had a near miss with him at the opposite end."

"We can't actually confirm that, Millicent. However, he has been seen dashing off in various directions."

Tom squared his shoulders. "He also drove in a reckless manner, endangering anyone who crossed his path."

"That's rather an exaggeration, Tom. We only witnessed his driving the one time. For all we know, it was the exception."

Tom stood his ground. "I'm inclined to think he made a habit of being a maniac on the road."

Millicent nodded. "Well... As I was saying, or about to say, I've asked one of the footmen to search the attics. I'm sure there is a box containing toy soldiers."

"Place cards and toy soldiers," Tom mused. "We'll crack this case wide open in no time."

Hearing the dowagers and Toodles approaching, Evie looked around the library. She didn't want to ring for Edgar, but they needed an alternative place to set up the rows of place cards. "Tom, would you mind bringing the card table from the drawing room? That should be big enough for the place cards."

Henrietta gasped. "Why is there dirt on the table?"

"Millicent, would you like to explain?" Evie stepped back. Turning, she pretended to study the contents of a bookcase. In reality, she was thinking about Señor Lopes.

Henrietta had only mentioned seeing someone, a man or a woman, with dark hair falling over his or her eyes. Of course, this didn't confirm anything. However, it did raise questions.

Had he attended church and why? Evie was sure there was a small church in the village near Althea's farm. Had he come out of curiosity? What if he'd had a specific purpose in mind?

When Tom returned with the card table, Evie sidled up to him and whispered, "The person standing near the pillar..."

"You're thinking it might have been..."

"Yes." *Señor Lopes*, she mouthed. "But why? We saw him today and he didn't mention attending the service or even visiting the village."

Tom straightened. "Well, he is a man of few words and quite fixated with directing those at you."

"What do you mean?"

"He compliments you a great deal."

"Are you jealous?"

"Me? Jealous of him?" In the next breath, he asked, "Do I have reason to be jealous?"

Evie wished the dowagers and Toodles would interrupt, but they had lost all interest in the place cards and were thoroughly intrigued by the model of the village Millicent was studiously constructing.

"Never mind all that," Evie joined the others.

"How marvelous." Picking up a leaf, Henrietta placed it in a strategic spot. "I believe that is the lane which intersects the main road coming out of the village. Do we have toy motor cars? We could use them to identify where the constables blocked the road."

Just then, a footman entered the library and set a box down on the desk. "These are the only ones I could find."

"We only really need one toy soldier," Millicent said. Rummaging through the box, she selected what she wanted and set it down on a patch of soil.

"Is that the vicar? Shouldn't he be lying down?" Henrietta flicked the toy and smiled. "That's better." Looking over her shoulder, she said, "Evangeline, does this look like the field where you and Tom stopped?"

Sara snorted. "She'll have to employ her imagination, Henrietta. Where are the wild flowers? Where's the grass? And the lane running alongside it is supposed to be lined with trees. You've traveled past that lane all your life."

Henrietta set about distributing the twigs and leaves along the lane. "Happy now?"

"Look what I found," Toodles said.

Looking over her shoulder, Evie saw Toodles inspecting the contents of the box.

"A toy motor car. Just what we need. Oh, here's another one."

Evie directed her to place one about to turn into the main road and the other one driving away from the village. Stepping back, she tried to remember what time she and Tom had driven by that field. It had been soon after luncheon and they had been on their way to Althea's house.

Tapping her chin, she mused, "Where did he go when he nearly ran us off the road?" The vicar's housekeeper hadn't mentioned anything about him returning to the vicarage.

Where had he gone and why had he returned?

By her estimation, there were at least two hours unaccounted for.

"Did Phillipa mention where she was driving when she had her encounter with the motor car that nearly drove her off the road?" Evie asked.

"She was headed here but I don't remember her being specific." Henrietta looked at the others for help but Sara and Toodles shook their heads.

Thinking about it, Evie realized the vicar could not have been responsible for nearly running Phillipa off the road.

"When did Phillipa arrive?"

"She arrived moments before we did."

"I don't see how the vicar could have driven off so soon after the service and reached the point where he nearly collided with Phillipa's motor. Phillipa must have arrived while you were all making your way back and the vicar was probably still talking to parishioners."

Tom tipped his head back and groaned. "That means we have another maniac driving around."

"We can definitely place him on that road next to the field where he was found."

Tom nodded. "Sometime after the service, he drove there and, for whatever reason, he drove off and nearly brought our lives to a premature end. Then, he returned."

"Oh... I just remembered something Mrs. Leeds said. After church, we went to visit Mrs. Higgins. Shortly after we arrived, Mrs. Leeds walked in and mentioned she'd just seen the vicar drive off. So he left soon after the service, after all."

Tom nodded. "And if he'd headed east, he would have encountered Phillipa."

"Yes."

Tom rubbed his eyes. "Then, later in the afternoon, he drove through the village again..."

Evie turned toward the table and studied the little tin man. When they'd had their encounter with the vicar, he'd been heading toward the village. Had he continued driving or had he stopped somewhere in the village?

Someone must have seen him.

"He must have spent the day crisscrossing the county. Going where?"

They all fell silent and studied the model of the village. This was interrupted when Edgar announced his presence by clearing his throat.

"Is luncheon ready?" Evie asked. "Well, I suppose we should take a break from all this." Glancing at the model of the village, she looked at the little tin toy again. It was lying face up. Thinking the vicar must have fallen forward, she leaned over and flipped it over, only to change her mind and turn it so it lay on its side.

Had the vicar returned there to meet someone?

Had he just been to the same field where he'd met his fate when they'd encountered him on the road?

Her imagination conjured a scenario where the vicar had gone there to meet someone only to find some sort of message saying there had been a change of plans. That's when he left, only to return later. If he'd found a message, had it been written? If there was a note, the police might find it and they would have a definite lead.

"Countess," Tom whispered, "you're making Edgar nervous."

She turned only to stop. "Millicent. You never said what you discovered about the vicar."

"Oh, dear. Didn't I?" Millicent rushed to the desk and found her notebook. "He's the Earl of Esterbrook's second son. I looked him up in Debrett's."

Evie closed her eyes.

"Countess?"

His housekeeper had said his family was well-to-do but she certainly hadn't mention anything about him being a second son of an earl.

"Mrs. Paterson said the vicar was going to be buried here. That strikes me as odd. If you recall, the house-keeper said the vicar's family was well-to-do. Now we learn his father is an earl. Why is the vicar being buried here?"

"There might have been bad blood between them," Tom suggested. "Or it might have been the vicar's wishes. Those are questions Henry will definitely be able to answer. I'm sure he'll want to speak with his family." Tom leaned in and lowered his voice to a whisper. "Edgar is about to start fidgeting. I think we should put him out of his misery and go through to lunch."

Evie whispered back, "Do you remember if Señor Lopes mentioned coming to the village? The question if plaguing me."

Tom shook his head. "He hasn't exactly been chatty with me." Smiling, Tom added, "If you wish to name him as a suspect, you will have my full support."

11

Casting aspersions

The dining room, Halton House

"Henrietta, are you feeling well?" Evie asked as they waited for the second course.

Henrietta's earlier excitement and interest in the model of the village Millicent was putting together had subsided.

While Henrietta had smiled and nodded at everyone's comments, she had remained quiet throughout the first course.

"Me? Oh, yes. Well, not exactly."

"Henrietta sounds muddled," Sara whispered.

"I heard that." Henrietta smiled at the footman who

approached and held a serving tray. As she helped herself to some potatoes, she said, "To be perfectly honest, I am still in shock over the vicar's death. The fact he has been killed is all I can think about because, as a matter of fact, he wasn't killed."

"Henrietta, I'm sure he is quite dead," Sara said.

"Sara, he was not killed, he was murdered." Henrietta gave a firm nod. "And before you claim there is no difference, I would like to argue the point. If a man dies from a gunshot wound inflicted on him accidentally during a hunting trip, we might say he has been killed. Hunting accidents have been known to happen. The vicar suffered a severe blow to the head." Henrietta shuddered. "It happened in a field. Lord Evans, or rather, Inspector Evans said... or perhaps it was Evangeline... Regardless, the discussion suggested the vicar was there to meet someone, and that someone planned the vicar's death." She looked at Evie. "Premeditation. Is that the correct term?"

"Yes, I believe it is."

"So that brings us to motive." Henrietta sent her gaze skipping around the table. "Who among us would have a reason for murdering the vicar?"

"Us?" Sara's eyes widened.

Toodles cut in, "What was he doing racing about the place? That's what I'd like to know."

Evie nodded in agreement. "His housekeeper said he was trying to become acquainted with the village and the surrounding area."

A footman lowered a platter and Toodles helped herself to some chicken. "That suggests he was interested in the architecture of the dwellings and the countryside.

I'm more inclined to think he was interested in meeting people. Specifically, the type of people who would appeal to an unmarried young man."

Henrietta's eyebrows curved up. "What are you suggesting?"

"I wouldn't be surprised if the vicar turns out to have been a veritable Casanova."

Henrietta nearly choked on her drink. "Do you mean to suggest he had been driving around seducing women? He'd only been in the village for a few weeks. Three weeks, to be precise."

"Let's think about it for a moment," Toodles suggested. "I can actually see him appealing to women."

"Not me," Henrietta declared.

Sara stifled a laugh. "I should think not. However, would you care to enlighten us? Who is your ideal type of man?"

"Sara, do I need to remind you of the breathless remark you made when you first met my husband, the 5th Earl of Woodridge? You were supposed to be agog over the prospect of being introduced to my son, the future Earl of Woodridge, and you couldn't take your eyes off my husband."

"Yes, but that was right before I turned and saw the future 6th Earl of Woodridge and, right after that, I never looked at another man."

Toodles smiled. "Ladies, let's not stray too far from the main topic. Someone caught the vicar's eye. Actually, by the sounds of it, it might have been several women. Would anyone like to hazard a guess as to the type of woman he might have found attractive?"

"As William Cowper expressed in his poem The Task, written in... let me think... Oh, yes. 1785..."

"Henrietta is about to lose her train of thought," Sara murmured.

Giving Sara a pointed look, Henrietta recited, "Variety is the spice of life, that gives it all its flavors. In other words, the vicar might have been quite indiscriminate."

"Well, I'm struggling to see him as a seducer," Sara admitted.

"Sara, you're not being helpful. We have already labeled him a veritable Casanova. Now, think. Someone in this village caught his eye."

Grinning, Sara suggested, "The woman wearing that jasmine scent."

Shaking her head, Henrietta mused, "That is not very helpful, Sara. No one here has been able to identify that woman."

Sara turned to Evie. "We could spend tomorrow searching for the scent. I purchase my scents in town, but the woman in question might have purchased her scent right here in this village."

"That is an excellent idea, Sara." How else could they discover the identity of the woman who had sat at the back of the church? Evie was about to take a bite of her chicken when she remembered Señor Lopes. If he had been at the service, he might be able to identify the woman. Although, his presence at church raised questions and he might, at the end of the day, become a suspect, quite willing to point the finger in another direction.

Evie glanced at Tom and realized she couldn't share her thoughts because she'd then have to admit to knowing Señor Lopes and that would risk exposing their secret prematurely.

"What if the vicar had been engaging in clandestine meetings with more than one woman?" Toodles suggested. "After all, that is the true nature of a Casanova."

"That would explain his wandering eye," Sara said and laughed. "Can you imagine that? The vicar engaging with his paramours right there in front of the entire congregation."

"Good heavens. It sounds downright indecent."

"Henrietta, you're just annoyed because you were oblivious to it. Just imagine, it was all going on right under your nose," Sara teased. "And you missed most of it because you were bedridden."

Toodles gave a woeful shake of her head. "I feel for the next vicar who takes over the parish. Henrietta will set spies on him to follow him wherever he goes, just so she doesn't miss out on any chicanery."

"All I can say is that the next vicar will have to be properly vetted. We can't allow our little village to fester under questionable spiritual guidance. I wouldn't be surprised if this one had a history and that's why we were stuck with him. For all we know, he might have been removed from his previous parish."

Evie assumed Henry Evans would be contacting the vicar's superiors to ask about his background.

"Henry definitely has his work cut out for him," Tom said. "It might be worth our while having another chat with the vicar's housekeeper. She was quite responsive today and might reveal more. Half the work seems to be in working out what questions to ask."

Sara appeared to be having a silent conversation with herself. Noticing this, Henrietta prompted her to share her thoughts.

"Well, I'm not entirely comfortable with the idea of sullying the vicar's name before we have all the facts. Speaking ill of the dead does not sit well with me."

"Are you afraid of being struck down by a heavenly wrath?" Henrietta shook her head. "My dear, we are merely trying to rectify a wrong by assisting the police in identifying possible suspects. The means justify the ends. Trust me, if we are committing an unpardonable sin, we will be exonerated."

"I don't see how. If our behavior and actions are unpardonable then that is the end of it," Sara argued. "There will be no exoneration."

Henrietta insisted, "Even a morally bad method justifies the ends."

Toodles smiled. "Well then... If we are going to sully his name, let's do it properly."

Henrietta rolled her eyes. "There's no need to be gleeful about it." Before taking a sip of wine, Henrietta asked, "Who would like to go first?"

Despite her reservations, Sara jumped in, saying, "He was the second son on an earl. Some people are actually in awe of someone with a title or even someone connected to a noble family. Can we assume he had used that as a lure?"

Henrietta's eyebrows shot up. "So much for your reluctance to smear the vicar's name."

Toodles tilted her head in thought. "I like the idea of him crisscrossing the countryside, captivating women by exploiting his noble connection."

"It all sounds so disturbingly sinister." Henrietta shuddered. "I will be both tantalized and repelled by the next vicar."

"Henrietta, that doesn't make sense."

"Sara, my dear, it is your failing and not mine. I could not have expressed myself more clearly. However, I will explain. At least, I will do so once you stop rolling your eyes. Now that the idea of a rakish vicar has been seeded in my mind, I will be highly suspicious of our next vicar and inclined to avoid his presence. However, I will also feel a strong compulsion to witness his debauchery in person."

Shaking her head, Sara complained, "This is all that woman's doing."

"Which one?" Henrietta asked.

"The one who wore the jasmine scent. If not for her, we would not have considered this deranged idea of the vicar having loose morals."

"I believe it was all triggered by the combination of the woman and the vicar's wandering gaze. As well as his mysterious jaunts around the place. It all adds up." Henrietta picked up her empty glass. "All this talking has made me thirsty."

"You might want to try listening."

"I had been content to listen until Evangeline questioned my silence."

Evie didn't know if she should apologize, so she tried to change the subject, but she couldn't think of anything that might intrigue everyone enough to distract them.

Instead, she sat back and thought about superficial certainties.

Everyone expected their vicar to display the highest

moral standards, behaving with unquestionable rectitude.

They had only now become aware of the fact the vicar had not settled in the village, fulfilling the usual obligations of a thoughtful and caring spiritual guide. Instead, he had gallivanted around, doing who knew what.

"Oh."

"Evangeline has been inspired."

"He made no effort to conceal his activities," she said.

Everyone gave her their full attention.

Evie went on to explain that as a second son of a nobleman, he would have enjoyed certain liberties. It was still unusual for someone with his background to seek some sort of occupation, but not entirely unheard of. Why had he chosen the path he had? Once upon a time, it would have been a given for a second or third son to join the church, but not these days.

Tom said, "What does that tell you about his character?"

"I'm getting ahead of myself. We're only discussing his activities because he was found dead."

"So you're saying that if he hadn't been killed, we wouldn't have become aware of his activities?" Tom asked.

"Perhaps in time. I couldn't really say. I suppose, eventually, people might have begun to notice. Mrs. Leeds certainly noticed something odd about his late-night arrivals."

Heavens. They had jumped to conclusions. And, as Sara had pointed out, this had happened because of a mysterious woman wearing a heady scent to church.

"If I hadn't been bedridden, I'm sure I would have

honed in on his questionable activities," Henrietta said. "My observations yesterday prove it. In fact, if not for my illness, I might have been able to prevent his murder."

"How is the view from up there, Henrietta?" Sara asked.

"It's a fine view, Sara. If I had to choose a spiritual animal, I am certain it would be the giraffe. They have the advantage of height and are forever vigilant."

Second sons, Evie thought, didn't bear the same weight of responsibility as the heir. That made his choice more difficult to comprehend. Joining the church seemed an odd choice for someone wishing to pursue a life of frivolity.

Evie's laughter drew everyone's attention to her. "We really should wait until we have more concrete information about him. So far, we have jumped to conclusions by leaps and bounds."

"Yes, and it has been highly entertaining. Ah! The pudding. Marvelous. I always enjoy a burst of energy after dessert. Should we all take a stroll to the village after luncheon? With any luck, we'll pick up the scent of jasmine and pin down the mystery woman."

"And then what?" Sara asked.

"Then, we subject her to an intense interrogation. Get the information out of her by hook or by crook."

"Grill her?" Sara suggested.

"Yes, indeed. I should make a note of that. Grill. It makes me think of tying someone up and holding them over a flame."

"And which arm of the police force empowered you with the right to do so?"

"I believe we have a citizen's right to question a suspicious character. But let's not quibble over minor details." Henrietta turned to Evie. "Will you and Tom be joining us on our mission?"

Oh, dear.

How would she get out of this one? Evie could feel her cheeks coloring. She had never mastered the art of lying and saw no great advantage in having to remember what one said.

Tom rushed to her rescue. "We promised to visit Althea."

Evie turned to him, her eyes wide, almost as if she'd been startled. "Oh, did we? Yes, we did. And we couldn't possibly go back on our word."

"I didn't know she'd come down from town. Why haven't you invited her." Henrietta looked to the others for support. "You've been entertaining so many people, I'm surprised. I thought you liked her."

"I do and that's why Tom and I are going to visit her. We're lucky she's making time for us. Althea mentioned something about enjoying the quiet country life." For someone not accustomed to lying, Evie felt she had done rather splendidly. However, a quick glance at Tom suggested otherwise as he studied her, his eyebrow raised slightly. She certainly recognized the look and thought she could almost read his thoughts.

Too much information, Countess.

12

*S*oon after luncheon, Tom and Evie set off on their drive to Althea Rawlinson's farm. Not bothering to hide her relief, Evie tipped her head back and smiled at the clear blue sky.

The steady flow of theories proposed during lunch had left Evie in a daze.

Everything they had discussed had been nothing but vague hypotheses, mostly constructed by their wild imaginations.

The method allowed them to entertain scenarios which led them to widen the scope of their investigation, such as it was. However, despite the gravity of the matter, this all remained a game.

The real investigation was being carried out by Lord Evans and they would have to wait until the end of the day to learn if he had discovered anything new.

He was working from a list and she assumed he was adding to that list. Had someone mentioned the verger?

Rodney Hale could not have been happy about his dismissal.

He had gone quietly.

If he had kicked up a fuss or expressed his resentment in any way, Evie believed word would have spread and someone would have mentioned it.

She glanced at Tom but didn't wish to distract his driving.

They'd forgotten to mention the verger at lunch. What would the dowagers and Toodles have made of the vicar letting him go without any clear explanation or, indeed, justification?

In the privacy of her own mind, she considered the obvious possibility. Being dismissed from a job he considered to be his whole life, Rodney Hale could have been driven to seek revenge. Could a man so dedicated to serving the local vicar bring himself to commit such a heinous act?

According to Mrs. Paterson, he had been dismissed from the role that gave him a reason to get up in the morning. The vicar had arrived three weeks ago and his first act had been to let the verger go.

Three weeks...

That would have given Rodney Hale ample time to build up a rage.

What explanation had the vicar given him?

Evie couldn't even begin to imagine the circumstances or the moment when the vicar ended the verger's livelihood.

Had the air crackled with tension?

If harsh words had been exchanged between the vicar

and Rodney Hale, Mrs. Paterson would have been there to serve as witness.

Evie stared into the distance, her eyes not blinking as she pondered a different scenario. What if Mrs. Paterson didn't want Rodney Hale getting into trouble?

Would she lie for him?

She'd be cunning, Evie thought. Yes, she would stick as close as possible to the truth but leave out the pertinent, incriminating details.

Don't say anything. Leave all the talking to me.

Evie entertained the one act play in her mind. She had no trouble seeing the entire village siding with the poor verger and conspiring to hide the truth and mislead anyone who came looking for answers.

Casting the vicar in a poor light would only help to divert attention away from the verger who no longer had a reason to get out of bed in the morning. For all she knew, the entire village had plotted against the vicar.

Feeling she had somehow overstepped the boundaries, Evie abandoned the idea of everyone contributing to a scheme aimed at diverting attention away from a possible suspect.

They needed facts.

Evie was convinced they would be able to establish a motive after they spoke with the vicar's family. In the next breath, she changed her mind and thought they would cast a bright light over his character, making sure his memory wouldn't be blemished.

Yet another conspiracy unfolded in her mind.

If they couldn't rely on the vicar's family for an honest appraisal, then they would have to look at his actions and decide for themselves.

Squaring her shoulders, she snatched the first thought that came to mind.

The vicar had wanted to clear the way, removing someone who might otherwise scrutinize his every move and, in the process, he made an enemy of the verger.

Shaking her head, Evie did some dismissing of her own and decided to stop thinking about the case. At least, until they had more concrete information, courtesy of Detective Inspector Evans.

Evie straightened in her seat and hoped their visit would offer a pleasant distraction. Her hope faded when she remembered they would want to question Señor Lopes to confirm his presence at church.

Evie leaned toward Tom and said, "We should tell Henry about Señor Lopes."

"Most definitely."

Sitting back, she turned her attention to the landscape and to Phillipa. She would be well on her way to her new life, opening a new chapter and filling it with one exciting experience after another. With any luck, she would read all about it.

As she continued to enjoy the surrounding landscape, she looked from one side to the other and, in the process, saw Tom looking at the rearview mirror, in itself nothing unusual, except for the fact he was doing it more often than he usually did.

This prompted Evie to glance over her shoulder.

She saw a motor car traveling at a safe distance behind them. She established this by looking over her shoulders a couple of times. Seeing the motor car maintaining the same distance, she realized it wasn't trying to race past them, something that would prompt Tom to slow down and give way.

"Do you recognize the motor car?" she asked.

"It's Henry."

"Do you think he's following us?"

Tom signaled ahead. "That's where we turn. I'll pull over then."

The motor car continued to maintain the same distance. Tom made the turn into the road leading to Althea's farm and stopped.

They both turned to see if the motor car followed them.

Less than a minute later, the motor drove by but did not slow or turn into the road. It simply continued on its way.

"It was definitely Henry," Tom said.

"Do you think he's headed toward the village?"

"He might be working on a lead. Remember, he spent the morning interviewing people. We've been focusing on the local people but the vicar was killed outside the village. It's possible he's found a lead to someone who lives in the next village."

"Do you remember what Clara Dalgety said about her sister, Margaret?"

He nodded.

"Mrs. Higgins told me Margaret Dalgety came to visit her. I'm sure she said this was three weeks ago."

Tom looked at her. "At the time the vicar arrived? Did Margaret Dalgety happen to attend the first service held by the vicar?"

Evie gave a tentative nod.

"Are we both thinking Margaret fell for the vicar?" Tom asked.

"It's possible."

"Do we know where she lives?"

"No, I didn't ask." Evie shook her head. "I don't know why I mentioned it."

"Unrequited love can be dangerous," Tom mused. "What do you think the dowagers and Toodles would say if they knew about Margaret's visit?"

"Well, if we also told them about her sister, Clara, fidgeting in church and looking rather anxious..." Evie groaned. "I believe they would have no trouble conjuring a scenario where the heartbroken Margaret decides if she can't have him then no one else will. That would be followed by another scenario where Clara seeks vengeance for the vicar's rejection of her sister, Margaret. Then, I would have to dissuade them of that theory because Clara Dalgety only left Mrs. Higgins' house to attend Sunday service." Evie hummed under her breath. "At least, that's what Mrs. Higgins told me. For all I know, she might be covering for her niece."

Tom laughed. "Just as well we didn't mention it at lunch."

They both stared into the distance.

"I hope he managed to catch up with Mrs. Leeds. When we spoke with her, she mentioned the jasmine scent. If her mind is anything like ours, she would have spent some time thinking about it until she finally remembered an essential detail. Or she might have come across someone she remembered sitting in the last pew who might have identified the mystery woman."

They both straightened and looked ahead only to simultaneously turn toward the left and look into the distance again. Lord Evans' motor car had disappeared from sight.

Evie spoke first, "The pub Señor Lopes is staying at is in the village up ahead."

"Chances are someone pointed Henry in that direction. But if someone mentioned seeing a foreign looking chap at the church, how would they know he's been staying at the pub?" Tom straightened again and looked ahead. "Theo will have arrived by now."

Heavens, she'd forgotten all about Althea's brother. She'd been looking forward to their visit but seeing Lord Evans and just now talking about Señor Lopes filled her with trepidation.

"He's waiting for our arrival."

Tom didn't need her to explain. "What are we going to do?"

During every single visit, they had jumped straight into their task, following Señor Lopes' instructions. On their last couple of visits, he had excused himself straight after their business concluded.

She remembered asking Althea about her first meeting with Señor Lopes. That had raised a few questions but, at the time, they hadn't really had any reason to be suspicious of him.

Before she could remind Tom of their conversation, he put the roadster into gear and got them on their way.

Within a couple of minutes, they'd reached the gate leading to Althea's farm. Slowing down, Tom drove through them and then sat back to enjoy the pretty scenery leading to the house.

When he brought the motor car to a stop, Evie

thought she could hear her heart thump all the way to her throat. "Have you come up with a bright idea? Do we broach the subject straightaway or wait for the right moment?"

"You just took the words right out of my mouth and, I should point out, I reserve the right to always ask for a prompt."

Sounding appalled, Evie asked, "Did you just throw the ball back in my court? How could you? We're both in this together."

Tom grinned. "I am a thoroughly modern man who has no qualms about deferring to someone more capable of making decisions."

"Fine. Brace yourself, Mr. Winchester, we are about to ruin a perfectly good afternoon by accusing our instructor of murdering the vicar, in a roundabout way, of course."

Tom's eyebrows shot up. "You're getting ahead of yourself. I thought we were only making tentative inquiries to confirm or deny a simple fact. Did he attend the church service or not?"

"Oh, yes, of course. But he's bound to ask why we wish to know. Also, I wouldn't be surprised if they've heard about the incident. Bad news always travels fast. He might have come up with a solid alibi, just in case."

Tom climbed out of the roadster and walked around to open the passenger door for her. "Of course, we could take the easy road and tell Henry where he can find him."

Before they reached the front door, Althea hurried toward them. "Be warned, the Theo you'll meet today is nothing like the one you met in London. You will see him in his element. He has descended into madness."

"Good heavens. Whatever do you mean?"

"At this precise moment, you will find him in the rear garden, measuring a hole large enough and deep enough to hold fish."

"Is he putting in an ornamental lake?"

"Yes! Right outside his bedroom window."

Instead of looking worried, Tom looked intrigued. "Point me in his direction. I want to see this for myself."

"Tom, we do have some other pressing matters..."

"Which you can tackle without me, Countess. I know you can." Tom swung toward the side of the house and sauntered off to meet Detective Inspector Rawlinson.

Althea pushed out a breath. "Hello. I suppose I should have started with that." She glanced over her shoulder. "This was my first opportunity to escape my unwanted guest."

"Oh, dear." Evie wondered how many more surprises Althea would spring on her.

"Petronella has been bedridden with a summer cold and now she is feeling better so, in her words, she meandered along a path and here she is. I would normally welcome her but Theo has me all flustered."

"Petronella? Why do I know that name?"

"I might have mentioned it when I reminded you of the dinner I'm holding." Althea looked heavenward. "I should have known better than to organize it. Theo is acting up because he didn't expect any guests during his stay." Althea closed her eyes for a moment. Pushing out a breath, she nodded. "I'm feeling better now and quite embarrassed by my display."

Evie laughed. "I'm sure that's how I react when the dowagers and Toodles get out of hand. Actually, I'm feeling fortunate not to have succumbed to that cold going around."

"Come inside and we'll have some tea. Señor Lopes has been trying to give Petronella instructions. That's another reason why she returned today. Oh, did I mention she stopped by yesterday?"

"No."

"Well, just as I was about to set off for the train station to collect Theo, along she came and I had a devil of a time trying to get rid of her. Don't get me wrong, she is lovely but, at twenty-five, still unmarried and expressing her irritation. Slim pickings, she calls it. You see, her father refuses to take her to town and she's stuck here for most of the year. That narrows her options, more so as she is reluctant to settle for just any man." Lowering her voice, she added, "I suspect she is trying to invite herself when I next go up to the town. I'm not sure I'm up to the task of chaperoning someone. Not that she would need it at her age but I would feel responsible for her."

Evie looked toward the house. "Have you heard about the vicar?"

"Reverend Peters?"

"No. I assume he's your local vicar."

Althea nodded. "A dear old thing. His voice drowns out the congregation. Sometimes, a few brave ones fight to have their singing voices heard but that only sets the vicar off. Which vicar are you referring to?"

"I was referring to our local vicar. The Reverend Jeremiah Stamford. He was found dead in a field. Now the police are investigating. In fact, Detective Inspector Evans, a family friend, is leading the investigation."

"So he was murdered? Whereabouts exactly?"

Evie described the field just outside the village.

"Oh, I believe I know that field. There are so many and yet that one stands out."

"Why?"

"There's an abandoned farmhouse opposite. I stopped there once to do some drawings. It's a solid building. I'm not sure why it's not used."

Evie thought she'd heard a rumor about the owners selling and moving into their house in town as a way to minimize their expenses. If she found herself in that situation, she honestly wouldn't know what she would do. On the one hand, remaining in the country meant having easier access to food grown on the farm. And on the other hand, country piles were notoriously expensive to maintain and run. She supposed the new owners didn't have any use for the farmhouse.

"And you say the vicar was found in the field?" Althea asked.

Evie nodded.

"What was he doing there?"

"We've been asking ourselves the same question." And, Evie thought, coming up with the wildest ideas.

They entered the library and were met by the strains of a familiar tune. Seeing them, Señor Lopes strolled to the table where the gramophone sat and lifted the arm, settling it down with studious care.

Althea proceeded to make the introductions.

Petronella Gladstone walked toward Evie, her hand stretched out. She had an easy, friendly smile and her eyes sparkled with amusement. She looked very smart in her beige cotton and linen clothes, perfect for a walk along country lanes.

Petronella cleared her throat. "How do you do? You must excuse my croaky voice."

Señor Lopes joined them. "You seem to be missing your other half."

"He'll be along soon, I'm sure."

"I trust you have been practicing."

"I'm afraid not but I can't imagine forgetting everything we learned overnight."

"Certainly not you, no."

Evie smiled at the suggestion Tom might have forgotten everything. In the midst of their lighthearted exchange, she remembered she was engaging a possible murderer.

It seemed incredible to entertain such a notion even if, only a short while ago, she had been suspicious of him.

"Have you been taking lessons from Señor Lopes?" Petronella asked, her voice breaking ever so slightly.

Evie found herself resenting the young woman's presence. How would she ever broach the subject she should be focusing on with Señor Lopes?

"Yes, for several days now. I do hope we are showing some promise."

Señor Lopes's response was interrupted by the sound of voices. Evie identified them as belonging to Tom and Theodore Rawlinson.

"Ah, wonderful. Tom has succeeded in coaxing my dear brother back inside. I fear his sudden enthusiasm for an ornamental lake will result in the house being flooded."

Evie turned to smile at the arrivals only to realize they were not alone. The presence of a third person was confirmed when Evie shifted her gaze beyond the door.

Tom entered and was followed by Theodore Rawlinson who greeted her with a hint of hesitation in his voice.

She hadn't seen him since their first encounter in town when he had been investigating a death. Evie imagined the detective had as yet to make up his mind about her. Although, she could see he'd had no trouble becoming chummy with Tom.

The person following them in should have been a welcome sight for Evie because his presence meant she wouldn't have to find a way to question Señor Lopes. However, she wished he hadn't arrived just yet. Now she felt as if she'd ambushed Señor Lopes or been in league with the police.

"Althea," Theodore drew his sister's attention. "This is Detective Inspect Evans. He's here to ask us a few questions."

Theodore introduced the others and invited everyone to sit.

When the detective explained his reasons for coming, Petronella Gladstone exclaimed, "Someone murdered the vicar?"

Evie studied Señor Lopes for any telltale reactions but his expression remained impassive. She would even go so far as to say it looked insouciant and wouldn't be surprised to see him shrug.

"I take it this is the first you heard of the incident?" Henry Evans asked.

Petronella shifted and looked at Althea. "Did you know about this?"

"Not until now."

Petronella pressed her hands against her throat.

"What a horrible thing to happen. Who would kill a vicar?"

"I believe that's what the detective is here to find out," Althea said and stood up. "I'm suddenly feeling very thirsty." She pulled the cord and her butler appeared at the door, almost as if he'd been hovering nearby.

"Withers, some tea, please."

Henry Evans dug inside his pocket and drew out his notebook. "Several people I spoke with say they saw a stranger in the village. They all described him as tall with dark hair and well dressed. Two of them said they saw him at church on Sunday." The detective looked at Señor Lopes. "Did you happen to attend the service on Sunday?"

Señor Lopes spoke without hesitation. "Yes, I did."

"Is that usual for you?"

"I'm not sure what you mean?"

"Forgive me for saying so, but I can't help but notice your accent."

Señor Lopes smiled. "And you wonder why I attended a Protestant service? My mother was English."

"I understand you are visiting and staying at the local pub."

"That is correct."

"The village has a lovely church. Why did you choose to attend the service at Woodridge?"

"I am visiting these parts and interested in seeing as much as I can. I happened to find myself driving through and when I saw everyone congregating outside the church, I decided to stop and attend the service."

"So that was the first time you'd been to the village."

"That is correct."

"You've been spending some time in this house."

At that moment, Evie knew the detective had spoken with Tom, who had obviously shared what little information he had at his disposal.

"I have been visiting Miss Rawlinson every afternoon."

"And what do you do with the rest of your time?"

"I have been enjoying the charms of the villages and surrounding landscapes. It is all a refreshing change from living in the city."

"And Miss Rawlinson is the only person you are acquainted with?"

"In these parts? Yes."

"How long have you been in England?"

Señor Lopes, who had remained standing, struck up a pensive pose. "Let me think. I can't be sure of the dates. I left Paris two months ago and spent a couple of weeks in the Riviera. I suppose I have been in England for just over a month, staying with the French Ambassador and his lovely wife."

"And how often do you come to England?"

"This is my first time."

"Before Paris, where were you?"

"I was in Barcelona and before that, in New York."

If Señor Lopes had been in England for a month, Evie imagined the detective would try to pinpoint a moment when he might have crossed paths with the vicar. The window of opportunity narrowed as the vicar had been in the village for three weeks. So, Señor Lopes would have to have met him during his first week in England.

"When you first arrived in England," the detective said, "where did you stay?"

"In London. At *The Ritz*. I was there for a week and then the French Ambassador invited me to stay with him and his lovely wife."

Evie almost forgot to breath. The questions were relentless and yet, somehow, the tone was kept conversational.

The detective held his gaze for a moment before asking, "And where will you be for the next few days or so?"

Señor Lopes shrugged. "I haven't really given it any thought. I suppose I'll still be here, staying at the pub. Summer is ending and I'm considering going up north for the grouse. I'm told I mustn't miss the Glorious Twelfth."

One of the busiest days in the shooting season referring to the twelfth of August, Evie thought.

The detective closed his notebook.

Evie could barely hide her surprise. To begin with, she didn't understand why he had chosen to speak with Señor Lopes in front of everyone. She also felt there had been several key questions he hadn't asked. One in particular stood out.

Had he ever met the Reverend Jeremiah Stamford?

To his credit, Señor Lopes had been cooperative and had remained calm. If he'd sensed he'd been interrogated, he hadn't shown any signs of resenting it.

Noticing she was still looking at Señor Lopes, Evie turned her attention to Henry Evans. However, as she did so, she noticed something else.

Petronella Gladstone was dabbing her nose with a white handkerchief. Or rather, she was holding the handkerchief up to her nose, almost as if she'd sensed a bad smell.

By staring as she did, Evie drew attention to herself.

Petronella lowered the handkerchief and smiled. "It's a trick my nanny taught me. The handkerchief is laced with peppermint oil." She signaled to her nose and waved the handkerchief. "It clears congestions."

Inhaling, Evie picked up the scent of peppermint.

Henry Evans stood up. Looking down at his notebook, he nodded and thanked Señor Lopes for his time.

Theodore Rawlinson walked him out, leaving everyone to stare at each other.

"I'm thoroughly mystified to say the least," Althea murmured.

"Yes, that was odd," Petronella agreed.

"Not necessarily," Señor Lopes said. "Someone saw me at the church and the detective obviously wanted to speak with me because I am a foreigner in these parts."

Petronella waved the handkerchief under her nose. "That's very understanding of you, Señor Lopes. In your place, I think I would be incensed. Anyone would think the detective suspects you of killing the vicar."

Señor Lopes smiled. "That is precisely what the detective thought and I don't blame him. He is only doing his job."

"I wonder who noticed you?" Petronella looked at Evie and then at Tom. "Were you at the service?"

"Yes, we were." Evie looked at Señor Lopes. "But we didn't see Señor Lopes." She, of course, refrained from saying the dowagers and Toodles had noticed a stranger with a lock of hair falling over his eyes.

"I'm afraid I did not notice you either, Lady

Woodridge. If I had, I would have made my presence known to you."

Evie thought she heard Tom growl under his breath.

"I don't quite understand why his presence at church matters," Petronella said.

"We can ask Theo when he returns," Althea suggested. "Being a detective, he's bound to know."

Petronella pressed the handkerchief to her nose. "Heavens. This is all so sudden. First, there was the news of the vicar and then poor Señor Lopes is questioned and clearly held under suspicion." She shook her head. "The poor vicar. Will there be some sort of memorial service for him?"

"A service is being organized," Evie said. "He's actually going to be interred here."

"Isn't that unusual?" Althea asked. "I seem to recall reading something in the local newspaper about the village having a new vicar. For some reason, I jumped to conclusions and assumed that meant he had come from another parish." Althea helped herself to more tea. "Did he have any family?"

Evie told them what little she knew.

"The second son of an earl. That's interesting. Do you think there's some history there? If anything happened to me, it wouldn't matter where I dropped dead, I know Theo would arrange to bring me back here. The Rawlinsons are all buried in the local church."

"We can only assume," Evie offered. And she hoped they would soon find out the facts. Glancing toward the door, she saw no sign of Althea's brother returning.

Señor Lopes stepped forward. "Shall we begin?"

Tom glanced over his shoulder toward the door. He

either wished to escape or prayed to be rescued by Theodore's return. Neither of which made sense to Evie. They had undertaken this exercise by mutual agreement.

They both stood up and as they walked toward the end of the room Evie asked in a hushed whisper, "What's wrong?"

"I'm intrigued by Henry's line of questioning and surprised he didn't take him in for further questioning."

His concerns were justified, especially as she had entertained a similar one. Henry Evans had fired one question after the other. She'd almost say he'd been merciless.

"I'm sure he has his reasons."

"Are we ready?" Señor Lopes asked.

13

----

*H*alf an hour later, they finished their lesson and Señor Lopes took his leave.

Petronella jumped to her feet. "Señor Lopes, are you driving back to the village?"

He held Petronella's gaze for a moment. After a significant, measured pause, he answered, "Yes."

"Marvelous. Can I beg a ride back, please? I'm afraid I exhausted myself coming here, even though I took the shortcut. I doubt I'd be able to manage the hill between our properties."

Señor Lopes inclined his head. "Of course. It would be my pleasure."

Petronella turned to them and, smiling, expressed her delight at having met them, then dashed off with a cheerful wave.

Withers showed them out and Althea waited until she heard the front door closing to say, "Well, that explains it."

"Explains what?" Evie asked.

"Petronella's enthusiasm for visiting me. She must have heard about Señor Lopes visiting here and decided to see for herself. I've never seen anyone look so entranced."

"Do you think she sees him as a catch?"

"She probably sees him as a ticket out of here. Her father is rather tight with funds. It's his way of exerting control over her. I don't actually blame him. I've heard a few rumors about her, nothing that can be substantiated, of course. Such is the nature of rumors."

"Is she difficult?"

Althea looked heavenward. "She's desperate. Who knows what sort of trouble she'd land in if she was let loose in town. Anyhow, Señor Lopes can look after himself." Althea stood up and excused herself. "I'll be back shortly."

As soon as they were alone, Tom murmured, "Bizarre."

"I actually find Señor Lopes' swift exodus strange too."

"How do you know that's what I was referring to?"

"Weren't you?"

"Well, yes..."

"There you go. We're headed toward that point where we can finish each other's sentences and read each other's thoughts. Anyhow, where do you think he's rushed off to?"

"Your guess is as good as mine, Countess. He must be going somewhere, otherwise, he would not have taken so long to agree to drive Petronella home."

"Yes, I suspect he had to rearrange his plans." He hadn't answered straightaway. In fact, his silence had risked turning into an awkward moment. "In the end, I think he saw taking Petronella with him as providing him with a solid alibi." Evie cleared her throat and, lowering her tone, said, "Detective, I was nowhere near that place. As it happens, I was right that minute driving Miss Petronella Gladstone home."

"Henry must be disappointed," Tom mused. "He had every single question answered, leaving him nothing further to pursue."

"I have unanswered questions. In fact, I'm still puzzling over his hurried exit. Yes, he's been leaving as soon as our exercises finished, but today was different. We're supposed to assume this was the first he'd heard about the vicar's death. You'd think he'd want to stay and discuss the incident, as well as Henry's questions. I find that very odd. Especially since he admitted to attending Sunday service." Evie closed her eyes and pictured him being questioned. He hadn't flinched once and he'd kept his attention fixed on Henry Evans. Nothing about him had suggested he'd been caught off guard. She'd almost go so far as to claim he had been ready. "Perhaps he wished to avoid our questions."

"We talked about Henry's interrogation and Señor Lopes didn't mind it. In fact, he accepted it."

Yes, Evie thought, but had he been expecting it?

Tom continued, "He might not be the dwelling type, or be interested in analyzing every single question."

"Heavens, listen to you. Defending your own?"

"My own?" Tom smiled. "Oh, yes. We men need to stick together."

What would a guilty person do?

Would they hide in plain sight?

It wouldn't be unheard of. The police had already been on the lookout for anyone suspicious lingering near the scene of the crime.

Evie walked to the sofa by the fireplace. With the days of sunshine and warmth numbered, it was a pity to see them spoiled by this dreadful incident.

As Tom joined her, she mused, "Once upon a time, I used to be quite blasé, never reading too much into anything, or making a mountain out of a molehill. Now I turn my attention to the slightest detail and blow it up into gigantic proportions." She glanced over her shoulder and toward the door. "He's staying at the pub. Do you think he already knew about the vicar's death?"

Tom snorted. "By now, news will have reached London and beyond. I'm sure he knew about the vicar's death."

"Althea didn't know."

Lowering his voice, Tom said, "She's had other things on her mind. Theo has been driving her batty."

Welcoming the change of subject, she asked, "Is he actually serious about the fish pond?"

This time, Tom laughed. "He threatened to divert the stream. Theo was actually looking forward to some peace and quiet and Althea sprung the dinner and a couple of social outings on him."

Looking up at the rows of books lining the walls, Evie mused, "I can't believe how calm Señor Lopes was throughout the detective's questioning."

"Ah, you've found something to chew on."

"Yes, I believe I am obsessing. I won't apologize for it. He's so composed, always oozing a calm demeanor. Does anything rattle him? There wasn't even the slightest lift of his eyebrow. I can't tell if he expected to be questioned or if he was taken by complete surprise." She closed her eyes and tried to think of other telltale signs that might have given him away. "A pulsing vein on his temple. A hard swallow. No, nothing. He didn't even shift or tense. The only time he hesitated was when he tried to remember where he'd been before coming to England. Then, he rattled off the information. Do you remember where we were a month ago?"

"In town dealing with a kerfuffle and other disturbances. Oh, and a murder."

"And if the police questioned you about the sequence of events? Would you remember it all as it happened?"

Tom groaned. "There would be a great deal of back and forth, toing and froing, remembering one incident and then being reminded of another. It would probably take me a while to piece it all together in the right order."

"There, you've just proved my point."

"I have?"

"It would take you a while to organize the sequence of events."

"And?"

"Señor Lopes had no trouble doing it. Admittedly, he took a moment to think about it."

"Yes, but he only had to remember staying at *The Ritz* and then being invited by the French Ambassador."

Evie hummed under her breath. She couldn't shake off the feeling it had all sounded rehearsed.

Tom stretched and crossed his feet at the ankles. "I look forward to hearing all about your findings."

Lost in her thoughts, Evie nodded, "I'm sure I'll have more questions than answers."

Althea returned and sat opposite them. "The session with Señor Lopes went rather well."

"Yes, I'm pleased with our progress. Actually, I'm rather surprised. My focus was on other matters."

"That's understandable. Theo has obviously chosen to remain outside, otherwise I would have asked him about all those questions. More tea?" Althea offered.

Accepting the offer, Evie turned and saw Theodore peering in.

He had a good look around the library and then, walking in, he flopped down on a chair. "I thought she'd never leave."

"Oh, dear." Evie shifted to the edge of her seat and was ready to stand.

"Theo. You're giving the wrong impression."

Looking up, he waved his hand. "Oh, do sit down. I didn't mean you. It's the strangest thing. When I'm in town, I can always find time to myself, even when Althea barges in. Then I come here and suddenly the house is swarming with guests hungry for company."

Althea shook her head. "Never mind all that. We have other questions."

"Theo, you walked Henry out. Did he share any interesting information with you?" Tom asked.

Theodore Rawlinson looked up in thought. "He's going back to Woodridge. There's someone else he wishes to speak with. Who was it... Let me think. Clare. No, Clara."

"Clara Dalgety?" Evie asked.

"Yes, that's the one. Someone saw her shoot to her feet and leave in a hurry at the end of Sunday service."

Evie explained at Clara needing to return to her aunt's house.

"She glared at the vicar," Theodore added.

"Glared?"

Theodore nodded. "The person who saw it said she'd looked almost as if she'd had a bone to pick."

What sort of grievance could Clara have against the vicar?

Evie thought back to what Mrs. Higgins had said about her niece, Margaret, visiting. Then there was her Clara's remark about her sister's condition only lasting until someone else caught her eye.

Had the vicar really caught Margaret's eye and did Clara hold the vicar responsible?

Theo went on to say, "He said to keep an eye on Señor Lopes. And that's another thing. I came here for peace and quiet and no work." He brushed a hand across his face. "Awful thing to happen. You don't expect people to be murdered right at your doorstep."

"Is he really a suspect?" Evie asked.

"He's a curious fellow. Henry Evans wants to find out more about him. Tom caught me up on all the news and told me there's a mystery woman who also attended Sunday service. Henry Evans didn't seem to know about her."

Belatedly, Evie realized they hadn't asked Señor Lopes if he'd noticed a woman sitting in the back pew. He'd given a reasonable explanation for being there. Had he been solely focused on the service or had he allowed his eye to wander?

"Anyhow, I'm sure Henry Evans will get to the bottom

of it all." He glanced at Evie. "Do you have any theories, Lady Woodridge?"

"We've been tossing about a few ideas but haven't come up with any suspects. Our theories are mostly based on a huge assumption." She explained how the vicar's penchant for driving around and returning to the vicarage late had led them to the obvious conclusion.

"Three weeks seems too short a time for him to have established himself as the local Casanova." Theodore frowned. "You say he's the second son of an earl. Do second sons still join the church?"

"We've asked ourselves the same question," Evie admitted. "I'm hoping Henry will find out something about his family. There might have been some sort of history between them. Maybe the vicar was cut off and had to find a way to earn a living."

That piqued his interest. "And the reason for that?"

Evie smiled. "I don't dare sully his name even further." Had the vicar seduced the wrong person?

The question settled in her mind as a reminder to bring it up when they returned to Halton House.

"Elizabeth Handicott found the body. She actually works for Sir George Gladstone. I wish I'd remembered earlier. I would love to have seen Petronella's reaction."

"What does she do?" Althea asked.

"I believe she works in the kitchen."

Althea snorted. "In that case, I doubt Petronella would know her. She's not the type to venture into the kitchen."

"Why are you interested in Petronella's reaction?" Tom asked.

Evie tapped her fingers on the armrest. "Did you

notice the cheery farewell she gave us? I might be reading too much into it but it struck me as indifferent."

Althea dismissed the observation with a shrug. "Some people are old for their age, showing a maturity beyond their years. Not so Petronella. I doubt marriage will change that."

"Regardless, I wish I'd mentioned Elizabeth Handicott." She looked at Althea's brother. "I'm sure you'd agree every bit of information is vital to the police who can then sift through it and decide what is and isn't relevant."

He nodded in agreement.

Evie told them about Edmonds being apprehended by the police and how earlier she had been thinking about the killer hiding in plain sight.

"Countess, are you about to suggest Elizabeth Handicott had something to do with the vicar's death?"

Before Evie could answer, Theodore said, "It wouldn't be out of the question."

Evie grinned at Tom. "There you go, and he is a real detective."

"So what is your theory?" Tom asked. "Elizabeth Handicott is engaged to be married. Why would she kill the vicar? Oh, wait a minute, are you about to suggest the vicar seduced her?"

"That hadn't occurred to me. However, now that you've mentioned it, they might have had some sort of liaison and..." Evie shrugged. "The possibilities are endless. He might have fallen for her and she refused to take him seriously so he threatened to expose her. She couldn't let that happen so she ended his life."

"And then lingered at the scene of the crime and

pretended to stumble on the corpse?" Tom didn't look convinced.

"We've questioned her presence in that particular field. It's certainly not the only one with wild flowers. What are the odds that she actually wandered along the one with a dead vicar? They must be astronomical."

"You're right," Tom conceded. "We haven't even begun to consider motives."

Smiling, Evie said, "That's because we've been waiting for some concrete information about the vicar's past. Hopefully, something to justify our current theory."

Althea looked at her brother. "What do you think?"

"A crime of passion makes sense. It's definitely a possibility but I say that with reservations based on the fact the vicar had only just moved to the village."

"And what does the detective think? Did he share any interesting information with you?"

"He's still interviewing people." Theodore steepled his fingers. "I've heard of Henry Evans but our paths have never crossed before. I hope he's open to your ideas."

Evie and Tom exchanged a smile. "He's been quite tolerant of us."

"What other theories have you come up with?" Althea asked.

Evie mentioned the verger.

Nodding, Theodore said, "Dismissed? That means he has a strong motive."

Standing up to pour himself some tea, Tom said. "For all we know, the killer could be an irate driver, fed up with the vicar's maniacal driving."

14

Althea saw them out, saying, "I look forward to seeing you again tomorrow. Please say you'll come."

"Of course, we'll come. We wouldn't dream of abandoning you," Evie assured her.

"Thank you. Theo will definitely appreciate the male company."

Evie gave her a conspiratorial smile. "It works both ways. Sometimes, I fear the dowagers and Toodles' antics will chase Tom away." Evie waved and as walked toward the roadster, she looked up at the clear sky and, for the briefest moment, forgot everything they'd talked about.

Tom held the passenger door open for her. "Well? Have you given it any thought?"

"Given any thought to what?"

"You were going to fixate on a thought. An idea."

"Oh, yes. That's right. I was thinking about Señor Lopes' smooth answers. He definitely didn't struggle with any of the questions. It's almost as if he'd boned up on the subject. Can we really assume he didn't know about the vicar's death? He didn't stay long enough for us to ask him."

"Would you have asked him such a pointed question?"

"I'd like to think I would have found a way to be subtle about it. However, I'm finding that the direct approach should not be dismissed."

"Because it can catch someone by surprise?"

"Yes. Oh, that's what Henry did. How very smart of him. Anyway, as I said, he appeared to have his answers all ready. Almost as if he'd had a contingency plan. *If the police question me, this is what I'll say.*"

"If he's guilty of any wrong-doing," Tom said, "he'd have to have nerves of steel to remain here, near the scene of the crime."

"And what's your point? Surely you agree he does have a steady manner about him."

"Steady? I'd probably describe it as suave, in a greasy sort of way."

Evie clasped her hands and tapped her thumbs together. "What if he knew the vicar had moved here?"

Tom grinned. "I'm listening."

Evie reminded Tom of that brief window of opportunity, that one week before the vicar arrived. Señor Lopes had been staying at *The Ritz*.

Tom walked around the roadster and climbed in. "Go on."

"Remember, the vicar is a second son of an earl. He must receive a tidy stipend from the family."

"And you think he enjoys the fine things in life."

Evie snorted. "Show me a member of the nobility

who doesn't. anyhow, Señor Lopes encountered the vicar and recognized him as his foe."

"I assume there is a past transgression somewhere?" Tom asked.

"Of course, but don't ask me what. Where was I? oh, yes... Señor Lopes heard the vicar was coming here. Then he met Althea and she told him where she lived, so he invited himself."

"Why do you think he was interest in the vicar?"

Evie sighed. "I suppose I could try to spin a tale about the vicar doing something to provoke Señor Lopes, but I'd struggle to think what that might have been. For the sake of argument, let's just say he had an axe to grind. He saw the vicar in town. He knew where he was headed but he couldn't follow him because that would have been too obvious. Suddenly, he sees his opportunity when Althea tells him where she lives. Now he has a credible reason for coming." Seeing Tom's eyes crinkling with amusement, she added, "I don't know why he had issues with the vicar. Something happened not long ago."

Tom chortled. "Maybe Señor Lopes has a sister and the vicar used all his Casanova charms to seduce her."

"Oh, heavens. I was hoping to empty my mind during the drive back. Just think. He could have been guilty and he could have been armed. We had a lucky escape."

"I thought we were embracing the idea of the vicar being a Casanova. At the first opportunity, we should find out if Señor Lopes has a sister." Tom put the motor into gear and they set off at a sedate pace.

As they assumed Henry Evans would still be busy interviewing people, they had no reason to rush back.

When they reached the corner where he had to make a turn, Tom leaned in. "Dare I ask?"

They should head back to Halton House.

Evie smiled and signaled to the left.

For the first few minutes, they had the road to themselves. Then a motor approached from the opposite direction. As it drove by, she and Tom glanced at the driver.

No one they recognized.

Evie focused on clearing her mind of all concerns and thoughts about the vicar, however, her mind found a replacement and filled her head with thoughts of Miss Petronella Gladstone.

Struck down by the same summer cold that had kept the dowagers and Toodles bedridden for over a week, she must have been desperate for company. What did she do the rest of the time? These days, one really needed to find some sort of occupation. Even if money wasn't an issue, the days could be long.

If her chances of meeting someone were slim now, the previous few years would have been more difficult. Even as war raged, people still managed to get on with their lives, finding joy wherever they could. Petronella must have been utterly miserable. Especially with so many men failing to return home. It wouldn't help if she had high aspirations.

Althea had mentioned hearing rumors about Petronella but she hadn't given any details.

Had she cultivated some sort of bad reputation? She would have come out at eighteen, well before the war. Had something happened to blemish her reputation?

Was that why she hadn't managed to find a husband?

Noticing where her thoughts had led her, she smiled and shook her head. At least she hadn't been thinking about the vicar's death.

Then she noticed something else. Tom had slowed down.

"What's wrong?"

He signaled ahead.

A motor car was just pulling into the road.

Tom slowed down even more and Evie understood why. At the speed he'd been traveling, if he didn't slow down, he'd drive straight into the other car.

Tom signaled up ahead again.

"What?"

"Look at where it was."

The field where the vicar had been found.

Was it someone curious to see the site for themselves?

"It looks like one of those Austin cars."

Tom nodded. "That's because it is."

The motor car finally picked up speed and began to put some distance between them.

Peter McCraw drove a car like it. Would Elizabeth Handicott's fiancé be interested in seeing where the vicar had been found?

If it was him, was he alone or was Elizabeth Handicott with him?

Mr. Howard was the other owner of a similar motor car. Evie asked herself the same questions. Was he alone or had he driven out to collect strawberries with Mrs. Leeds?

Another possibility occurred to her.

What if it was the killer, returning to the scene of his crime?

Evie glanced at Tom. He'd brought the roadster up to normal speed and they were gaining on the other motor car. Did he plan on following it? His expression looked determined, with his gaze fixed on the vehicle ahead of them.

He turned to her. "Should we follow?"

It wouldn't hurt. Although, she didn't see the point to it. When they discovered the identity of the driver, what would they do? Question them? On what authority?

Evie remembered they knew of another person who drove that model motor car.

Margaret Dalgety.

When Peter McCraw had stopped at Mrs. Higgins' house to collect Elizabeth Handicott, Mrs. Higgins had said she'd thought it might have been her niece, Margaret, because she drove the same motor car.

They arrived at the village and had to slow down. Tom maintained a safe distance, although it was close enough for Evie to see there were two people in the motor car.

When they turned into a familiar street, she decided the driver had to be Peter McCraw and his passenger, Elizabeth Handicott.

Slowing down to make the turn, Tom said, "The car's headed for Mrs. Higgins' house." He brought the roadster to a stop near the corner. "Well? Do you wish to speak with them?"

Evie saw Elizabeth Handicott climb out of the vehicle. She was carrying a bouquet of flowers. "By the time we reach her, she'll be inside. What possible reason could we give for visiting Mrs. Higgins again?"

A motor car drove by and stopped in front of them.

"Is that Henry Evans?"

Tom tipped his hat back. "Yes, it is."

Henry Evans climbed out and approached them. "I was about to drive back to Halton House when I spotted you. Is there anything I should know?"

Tom nudged his head toward the motor car parked in front of Mrs. Higgins' house. "We saw them stopped at the field and wanted to find out who the driver was."

Without turning to look, Henry Evans seemed to know whom he was referring to. "I spoke with them earlier and they mentioned wanting to collect some flowers but, given the circumstances, they weren't sure if they'd be allowed to."

"And you gave them your permission?" Evie asked.

Henry Evans nodded. "I saw no harm in it. Although, if you ask me, it's rather ghoulish to still want to use flowers from that field for a wedding bouquet." He smiled at them. "What did you think they were doing? Returning to the scene of the crime?"

"It's a reasonable assumption. I don't know about Tom, but I wanted at least one question answered today. And now I've thought of another one. You told Theo Rawlinson someone had seen Clara Dalgety rushing out of the church."

"Yes, Mr. Brown. He owns a store. He usually sits in one of the back pews because he prefers to avoid the line. He thought Clara Dalgety's behavior looked odd."

Mr. Brown?

Evie looked at Tom.

They'd spoken with him and he hadn't mentioned anything. After all the trouble they had gone to, coming up with a reasonable explanation for going in to his store...

"Did you follow up on it?" Evie could have spared him the trouble.

"I did. In fact, that kept me busy for a good hour. First, I had to get through Mrs. Higgins and her friend, Mrs. Leeds, who had just dropped by for a visit. Long story short, I ended up driving out to speak with Clara's sister."

"Really? How did that come about?" She'd been thinking about Margaret Dalgety only a few minutes ago.

"Clara Dalgety had been incensed by the vicar. That's how she explained her behavior. Apparently, he'd been quite rude to her sister who'd been nothing but welcoming. On Sunday, she waited until the final blessing and, while everyone still remained seated, she shot to her feet and stormed out. That was her way of expressing her disdain."

"And what did Margaret have to say about it all?"

"She admitted to a foolish infatuation with the vicar. She actually referred to it as a *coup de coeur*."

Loosely translated as a strike or a blow to the heart, Evie thought. A moment of intense and inexplicable feelings that brooked no argument and listened to no reason. And it had happened in a short span of time. She'd visited her aunt at the time of the vicar's arrival. Had he spurned her?

Henry Evans stood next to the roadster, looking around them. "It's the perfect motive," he said with regret.

"Did she attend Sunday service? I'm guessing she didn't and..." Evie's thoughts drifted.

Soon after the service, the vicar had driven off. Mrs. Leeds had confirmed it.

Later, she and Tom had arrived back at Halton House and Phillipa had been there with a story about nearly being driven off the road. They had no way of verifying it, however, Evie was sure the vicar had been the culprit.

Evie signaled to the road leading out of the village. The road which everyone took if they were headed to London.

"Does Margaret Dalgety live out that way?"

Henry Evans nodded.

"She wasn't at the service on Sunday," Evie mused.

Again, he nodded. "She told me the vicar went to see her after the service."

"Did she say why?" She hadn't been at the service and, Evie was sure, he hadn't been tending to his flock because Margaret didn't belong to this parish. Nor did her sister, Clara. The vicar had actually gone out of his way.

"She gave me an explanation but I didn't actually believe it." Henry Evans looked down for a moment. "She said the vicar wanted to apologize for his abrupt manner during their first encounter."

"And you think Margaret lied?" Evie watched Henry Evans expression for any telltale signs. He appeared to be debating with himself, his gaze shifting around, the edge of his lip twitching. He shifted and then straightened.

"When I asked her about it, she paused. She was about to answer when she paused again. That's always a sign of someone either changing their response or adjusting it in some way."

"The vicar probably wanted to stop her pursuit of him," Tom suggested.

"That would be my guess," Henry Evans agreed. "And I doubt he was polite about it."

"Is that something you've come to realize after talking to the villagers?" Tom asked.

"No one has come straight out to say it, but I've been getting the feeling the vicar didn't really have much time for his parishioners."

Evie thought Margaret Dalgety had appeared to do a good deed by not besmirching the memory of a man who'd been killed. In fact, Evie was inclined to believe Margaret had wanted to spare herself further embarrassment.

"Do you believe Margaret had motive?" Tom asked.

Henry answered with a smile. "Oh, yes. Absolutely."

Both Evie and Tom's eyebrows lifted.

"But she has a solid alibi," he added. "After the vicar's visit, she went to her neighbor's house and spent the afternoon making jam. Her job was to wash the jars. She broke one and cut herself badly enough to need the local doctor to tend to it."

"And you confirmed all that?" Tom asked.

Henry Evans nodded.

Evie's shoulders lowered. "Well, at least you've crossed one suspect off the list. Who else remains?"

When Henry Evans didn't respond, Tom smiled at Evie, "Nice try, Countess. It seems the detective wishes to keep his cards close to his chest."

Evie harrumphed. "We crossed Clara off the list."

"Really? I spoke with Mrs. Higgins and her niece, and I walked away thinking Clara Dalgety was hiding something and her aunt was covering up for her."

"To be fair to Evie," Tom said, "she reached the same conclusion."

Shaking her head, Evie murmured, "The villagers didn't have enough time to collude. If Clara dashed out in the afternoon, someone would have seen her. There were too many people out and about. It would have been impossible for her to go unnoticed. No, she did not kill the vicar."

Henry Evans looked at his watch. "Time is running out and I'm coming close to lodging my findings. It looks like the case will remain unsolved." Henry Evans' attention was drawn to a motor car driving by. "I believe the vicar's family has arrived. The service is due to be held tomorrow."

Evie swung around in time to see a fancy motor car heading toward the vicarage.

Stepping back, Henry Evans adjusted his hat. "I'll give them half an hour to settle in."

Evie shifted in her seat.

Seeing her look of eagerness, Henry Evans shook his head. "No, absolutely out of the question. You cannot be present."

With a smile and a wave, Henry Evans walked to his motor car and drove off, leaving Evie and Tom to ponder their options.

"I suppose we should head back to the house." Evie pushed out a breath filled with frustration.

"Cheer up, Countess. The dowagers, Toodles, and Millicent might have solved the case and are right this minute asking Edmonds to set out in search of us."

15

*E*vie searched through her handbag.

Returning to Halton House was out of the question.

"Oh, what did I do with the address Mrs. Paterson gave us?"

Tom dug inside his coat pocket and retrieved a piece of paper. "Is this what you're looking for?"

"Thank goodness. I was sure I'd taken it."

Tom drew in a deep breath. "I suppose this means we are not going home."

Evie shook her head. "No, not just yet. We should have mentioned Rodney Hale. Why didn't we?"

"Because we were busy discussing Margaret Dalgety."

"Yes, I'm afraid we've only heard half the story. She is definitely keeping the interesting bits to herself."

"All for the sake of cherishing the vicar's memory?" Tom laughed.

"No, I think she'd want to spare herself the embarrassment." She looked ahead, her eyes not blinking. "Yes, we should pay Rodney Hale a visit."

"And if Henry objects?"

"When we see that bridge, we'll... I don't know. I'll think of something."

Tom got them on their way. "It's at the end of the street heading out of town. Not far from here. And, if Mrs. Paterson is to be believed, we will find him at home."

"Yes, but will he open the door to us?" Going by what Mrs. Paterson had said, Rodney Hale had been left devastated by the dismissal.

They found his cottage on the edge of the village. In keeping with the rest of the cottages, his garden displayed an abundance of blooms, with not a single weed in sight..

"The front window is open." Evie pointed at the curtain fluttering in the light breeze. "That's a good sign."

They walked up to the cottage and Tom opened the little gate. Knocking on the front door, they stepped back and looked toward the window in time to see a cat peering at them.

To their relief, the front door opened.

Rodney Hale lowered his head and stepped out, just barely avoiding the door frame. "My lady?"

To this day, Evie continued to be surprised when someone addressed her by her title. Indeed, she was surprised anyone recognized her.

Tom and Evie greeted him.

"I hope we haven't caught you in the middle of something." Evie glanced at his garden and remarked how pretty it looked.

Rodney Hale surprised her by saying, "You're here to ask me about the vicar."

Evie nodded. "Has the detective spoken with you?"

Rodney Hale looked away and into the distance before saying, "No, but I've been expecting him. To be honest, I'm surprised he hasn't come by. Perhaps he's been leaving me to stew in my own juices."

"Why do you think he'd do that?"

He shrugged. "I'm sure you know the vicar dismissed me. That means I have a motive." Smiling, he added, "I read detective novels." He stood aside and invited them in.

He kept his cottage neat and tidy. He was clean shaven and had run a comb through his hair. His shirt looked freshly ironed and his shoes polished. Evie decided Mrs. Paterson had exaggerated. Rodney Hale clearly had no trouble getting out of bed. Either that, or he had found another reason to live.

His gray and brown tabby sauntered up to him and settled between his feet. Picking him up, he cradled the cat in his large hands and offered them some tea.

"Thank you, but we really don't wish to take up too much of your time." She imagined Edgar waiting for them to return, his hand itching to ring the dressing gong.

"You wish to know what happened," Rodney said.

"We've heard Mrs. Paterson's version of events. It seems the vicar gave you no reason for dismissing you."

"That's right, my lady. And I didn't ask for a reason."

"Why not?"

He looked down at his shoes. "Sometimes, you just know."

Evie puzzled over that.

"Some people call it a knack," he explained. "I just

look at a person and just know." He shrugged and added, "If they're good or bad."

Evie and Tom leaned in slightly, both eager to hear Rodney Hale's verdict.

"He was neither. That's what I sensed."

"You mean, you sensed some sort of lack?" Evie asked.

"Yes, I suppose you could call it that. He just didn't seem to care." He frowned. "Perhaps that's not right. I had the feeling he was on the lookout, never really here, in this moment."

"As if he was looking ahead for the next opportunity?" Or thinking of some other place he'd rather be...

"Yes." Again, he shrugged. "I might be right, or I might be wrong. I just couldn't shake off the feeling he had no time."

No time?

She remembered Mrs. Leeds asking Mrs. Higgins if the vicar had visited. He hadn't, and she'd walked away thinking she would need to have a word with him.

"And you didn't mind leaving the position?"

"Oh, I did, but I just didn't see the point in making a fuss. I told myself he wouldn't last, and he didn't."

Rodney Hale had every reason to dislike the vicar. She tried to picture the tall man with straight shoulders making his way out of the village to meet the vicar and deliver the fatal blow.

Shaking her head, she smiled at him. "There'll be a new vicar soon and you will be reinstated." She'd definitely see to it. "By the way, did you attend Sunday service?"

Rodney Hale shook his head. "I went to the next village. The reverend there has a booming voice. It always drowns out everyone's singing. I find that amusing. You see, it turns into a competition to see who can sing louder than the vicar."

"The Reverend Peters?"

"Yes, that's the one."

So Rodney had traveled along the same road they had in the afternoon.

"Did you return here after the service?"

"As a matter of fact, no, I didn't. I have some friends there and they asked me to stay for lunch. We had some catching up to do, so lunch turned into afternoon tea."

"And did you drive there?"

"Only just."

"What do you mean?"

"My motor car has seen better days. I try to avoid hills because I know it's just asking too much of it."

He would have driven by the field late afternoon. "Can you recall what time it was when you returned?"

He looked down at his cat. "No, not precisely. But I do recall driving by the field everyone has been talking about. Actually, I even remember seeing Elizabeth Handicott standing by the side of the road. I almost stopped to see if she needed help. I saw her clambering up and she seemed to then walk with purpose."

"So you actually stopped."

"Yes, but only briefly. When I saw her bend down to pick up some flowers I realized she'd meant to be there. That's when she saw me."

"She saw you?"

"Yes, she waved and I waved back. Then she went back to picking her flowers, so I drove off."

In other words, Rodney Hale had an alibi. Plenty of people had seen him in the next village.

He set his cat down and straightened. "I've been giving it all some thought. By now, enough information has trickled down and all I need to do is step out for a brief walk and I encounter someone who'd just spoken with someone... Anyway, it seems the vicar might have been killed shortly before I drove by." He shook his head. "It's the strangest thing because I just don't remember seeing anyone else on the road behind me or coming in the opposite direction. Elizabeth Handicott is the only person I encountered there and I know she gets someone to drive her back from her job."

Had the killer lingered somewhere nearby? Waiting for the perfect moment to make his escape?

The farmhouse.

That would have offered a perfect hiding place.

"Do you happen to know how Elizabeth Handicott raised the alarm?" It was something that only now occurred to Evie.

"I believe she walked, ran and hobbled to the village."

There, Evie thought. Right there. That's when the killer must have made his escape.

They thanked him for his time and assured him he wouldn't have anything to worry about because Detective Inspector Evans was a reasonable man.

"If you say so, my lady. Although, in my experience, those types are few and far between."

16

Halton House

om smiled to himself. "Every time we return, I see the house and think... Halton House, or what remains of it."

"You've never told me and what do you mean?"

"I take my prompt from something you said once about always being surprised to see the house still standing."

Evie laughed. "Yes, well... Let's never bring out the gunpowder. I would toss and turn, worrying about what the dowagers and Toodles might do with it."

A feeling of contentment swept through Evie. She'd had the good fortune to marry Nicholas, whom she'd adored. Enjoying every moment of his company had been a blessing. And now she'd been gifted with another chance.

Tom leaned forward. "I see Edgar standing at the door. That can't be a good sign."

"Oh, dear." Evie straightened her hat and hugged her handbag to her chest. "I should have brought Holmes with us. He can be very comforting in my moment of need."

"Any last words before we're bombarded with whatever has been going on in there?"

Once they stepped inside, Evie knew their train of thought would be completely derailed.

"Let me think."

"Quick, Countess. We're getting closer."

"Trust you to turn this into a game." Evie thought about the last person they'd visited.

When they'd left Rodney Hale's cottage, they had walked back to the roadster in silence. Even as they'd settled in to drive back, they hadn't said much.

"Well, I'm glad we finally caught up with Rodney Hale."

"Can we believe everything he said?"

"The thought didn't even cross my mind. Is that a failing? Have I been gullible? No, I don't think so. In fact, if we spoke to every single person living in the village, they are all going to vouch for Rodney Hale. Even those who don't know much about him."

"Because he's never made any trouble?" Tom asked. "Those people are usually the ones who could easily get away with murder."

The verger had been able to account for his whereabouts and, if required to, would be able to provide witnesses to confirm his location at the time of the murder.

"Elizabeth Handicott saw him," Evie reminded him. A moment later, she looked up at the sky and groaned. "What if..."

Tom laughed. "You're picturing him leaving his motor car somewhere out of sight, walking to the field, meeting the vicar..."

Evie nodded. "If he'd left the motor car by the side of the road, Elizabeth Handicott would have seen it. So, you're right. He might have left it out of sight. Except... there is no other road or lane for quite a distance. It would have been a long hike." She drew in a breath and pushed it out. "No, we mustn't try to find a reason to doubt him. Besides, we can't overlook the fact he has a multitude of people who'll vouch for his whereabouts."

"A multitude?"

"Yes, a multitude. Starting with the villagers from Woodridge. According to Mrs. Paterson, he hasn't been out of the house since losing his position as verger. I'm sure she's not the only one who noticed this. Mark my word, the moment he set foot outside his house, everyone took notice."

"So we don't have a suspect."

"We're not looking for a suspect. We're looking for the killer." Evie thought she heard Tom say she'd wanted to stay several steps behind the detective. "I changed my mind. What if an innocent villager is hauled to prison? We can't let that happen. We won't." Evie pointed ahead. "Let's get this over and done with."

"That almost sounds like a battle cry." Tom laughed and hurried up the drive.

Edgar walked toward them, his shoulders back, his head lifted. "My lady. Mr. Winchester."

"Edgar, I hope we haven't kept everyone waiting."

"Not at all, my lady. Everyone is still ensconced in the library. It might take your persuasion to shift them out of there."

"Have they been busy building the little village?"

Edgar's face tightened.

Aha. Evie believed she had just hit upon Edgar's bone of contention.

"If anyone had bothered to consult with me, I could have pointed them in the right direction. We have a battlefield model in the attics. I'm sure it would have served the purpose. Instead, the library is now filled with soil from the garden. At one point, Holmes jumped off Lady Sara's arms and landed on the model. He made a veritable mess of it all and then proceeded to trudge through the library leaving dirty paw marks all over the floor and carpets. The library will have to undergo a thorough clean."

"And Holmes? Has he taken cover somewhere?"

"He is currently being bathed, which, of course, means two of the housemaids will then have to change their clothes because he would have done a thorough job of getting them wet."

Evie looked at her watch. "I take it you wish to ring the dressing gong."

"At your signal, my lady."

"I believe that will be enough to stir the others away from the library."

"Very well, my lady." Edgar swung on his feet and made his way back inside.

"Shall we go see what the others have been up to?" Tom asked.

"I'd rather not. Let's hurry inside and up the stairs. I'd prefer to be washed and changed first."

"You realize that means they'll be revitalized and ready to assail us with their accounts of the afternoon."

Evie smiled. "Yes. By then, however, I will have a glass of brandy in my hand."

～

An hour later

"What a day." Evie emerged from her boudoir feeling fully refreshed and ready to tackle the evening. There had been a knock at her bedroom door but she had asked Millicent to ignore it. The number of footsteps they'd heard scuttling away had told them all they'd needed to know. The dowagers and Toodles had tried to have a word with her.

Walking to her dresser, she selected a pair of earrings and was about to compliment Millicent on the fine job she had done with the little village when she remembered she hadn't mentioned the letter she had received from Merrin.

By now, of course, Millicent would have heard all about it.

She glanced up and caught Millicent as she turned toward her. She had been frowning but, at the last minute, managed to replace the expression with a smile of contentment.

"Millicent, about Merrin..."

"I've heard the news, milady. I can't exactly say I'm

thrilled or pleased. She never said anything about being unhappy or having any issues with the other servants. Not that she would because we are all perfectly lovely." Her shoulders rose and fell. "I liked her and, if truth be known, I'm hurt." She held out an evening dress in a deep shade of green with an embroidered panel.

As Evie slipped into the dress, she wondered what they would do now. "We'll have to find someone new."

"Perhaps we should wait a while, milady. There's no point hurrying this. Besides, I'm perfectly happy to juggle my duties. There might be someone from the village. She wouldn't have to have experience. I could train her."

Train and shape her?

Evie smiled. "I'll leave it up to you, Millicent."

"Did you have any luck today?"

Evie told her everything they had learned along the way. "We met the verger, Rodney Hale, and found him to be quite lovely. Oh, and during our visit to Althea Rawlinson we met Petronella Gladstone. I must remember to ask Althea about her history. She mentioned something about rumors but I didn't ask for details." She glanced at Millicent. "Do you think you could see what you can find out about her? She lives in the next village."

"Rumors," Millicent hummed. "Does that mean she might have a reputation?"

"I think so, yes."

Millicent nodded. "I'll see what I can find out."

Evie sat down at her dresser and Millicent went to work on her hair.

"I'm not going to ask about this afternoon because I know they are all simply bursting to tell me but if there is anything of significance..."

Millicent shook her head. "I'm sure they wanted to see you because they were eager to find out if you had discovered anything new. They behaved well enough. I set them the task of making the little village pretty."

"By the way, how is the poem coming along?"

Millicent's cheeks colored. "I wonder, by my troth, what you and I did, till we loved."

"Marvelous. Well done, Millicent." Evie glanced at Millicent's left hand as she had been doing since their return from town.

Still no ring.

She knew Edgar had purchased one but she didn't dare ask about it.

All in good time, she supposed.

The drawing room

Walking in to the drawing room, Evie heard Henry Evans say, "The funeral service will be held tomorrow."

Tom approached her, a glass in hand. "I think you'll need this, Countess."

Taking the glass from him, Evie held it up to her lips and sent her gaze skating around the room.

The dowagers and Toodles sat on a sofa, their attention fixed on Henry Evans.

It only took her a moment to realize they were all ignoring her.

Oh, dear...

Looking at Henry Evans, Evie asked, "Did I hear you say the service will be held tomorrow?"

"Yes, the vicar's family is eager to get it over and done with."

"I take it those are not your words."

"No, they are not. What does that tell you about the vicar's family?"

"Do I dare to jump to conclusions?"

"I think, in this instance, you should."

"So it's official. The vicar was not on good terms with his family."

"A bad seed. That's how his father referred to him when he thought I was out of earshot. His parentage was questioned by the earl's heir. Of course, they were all apologetic. I don't know if they are perfectly dreadful and not afraid to express their disdain or if I caught them in a moment of grief and unable to contain themselves."

"Heavens, do you think we'll all be a welcome distraction for them tomorrow?"

"To be perfectly honest, I think they will be surprised to see anyone turn up at the service."

Henrietta snorted. "They obviously underestimate people's curiosity. Everyone will be keen to see for themselves. It will give them something to talk about for a day or two."

Evie nodded. "I'm also interested to see for myself." It surprised her to hear they had no inhibitions and expressed their disdain so freely.

"Just as I was about to leave," Henry continued, "the strangest thing happened. You will never guess, so I'll tell you. Miss Petronella Gladstone waltzed in. She'd been on her way to a dinner in the next village and decided to stop and see how Mrs. Paterson was getting on. So imagine her surprise when she was told the family had arrived. Of course, she had to pay her respects in person." Henry Evans took a sip of his drink. "It took her next to no time to become quite friendly with the earl and his son."

"Who else was present?" Evie asked.

"The vicar had a sister and, of course, his mother was there. She didn't say much. His uncle was also there and a couple of cousins. I'm actually surprised they were able to gather together so many members of the family at such short notice."

"Perhaps they were expecting this outcome," Sara suggested.

Henry Evans sat forward.

Tom studied his glass as he said, "Now, there's an idea. Do you think his family wanted to be rid of him so badly they organized to have him killed?"

Sara gave him a brisk smile. "Worse things have been known to happen."

"What an odd family," Evie whispered.

Edgar appeared at the door and gave a nod to indicate dinner was ready to be served.

"Shall we go through?" Evie invited and led the way in.

As they took their seats, Sara murmured, "We are always so uneven. Too many women, not enough men."

"I rather enjoy outnumbering the men," Henrietta replied. Tasting the entrée, she expressed her delight. "This fish mousse is delicious. I almost feel wicked savoring such a delightful dish while talking about some-one's death."

Henry Evans glanced toward the door.

When he did it again, Evie asked, "Is something wrong?"

He smiled. "Not at all. I just... Well, a part of me expects Caro to burst in at any moment. Of course, she won't because she doesn't even know where I am."

"The distance is quite manageable. She might decide to pay us an impromptu visit," Sara suggested.

"Detective..." Henrietta shook her head. "Henry. You were telling us about this young woman who burst in on you at the vicarage."

He nodded. "Miss Petronella Gladstone. Her father is Sir George Gladstone. Do you know him?"

"No, I can't say that I do. Perhaps he's only recently been knighted."

"I'm afraid I couldn't say. Anyhow, when I left, Miss Gladstone was still at the vicarage becoming better acquainted with the family."

"Do you think they minded?" Henrietta asked. "I think I would find it odd to have a complete stranger imposing on my moment of grief."

"They didn't appear to. In fact, I think they were glad of the distraction. She seemed to cheer them up."

"And you said you met her at Althea Rawlinson's house." Henrietta glanced at Evie before turning her attention back to her entrée, her lifted eyebrow expression suggesting she had opinions she wasn't sharing with them.

"Yes." Henry Evans turned to Evie. "Does she visit regularly?"

"Not that I know of."

"How would Evangeline know?"

"Althea might have mentioned it," Tom suggested. "In fact, she mentioned a rumor, but Evie doesn't know the details. We were eager to return."

Looking up in thought, Henrietta said, "You mentioned someone else but you were distracted by Toodles asking a question."

"Should I apologize?" Toodles asked. "I feel I should. Never mind, I won't apologize because that will take us off course again and we do want to hear about this other presence at Althea Rawlinson's house."

Her granny shot her a look filled with challenge.

Oh, dear.

They knew.

But what did they know?

"Henry?" Henrietta prompted.

"Oh, yes. I'd been interviewing people and a couple of them mentioned seeing someone they didn't recognize at Sunday service."

"Fascinating," Henrietta murmured and turned to Sara. "Isn't that fascinating?"

"Yes, it is." Sara turned to Toodles. "Do you find it fascinating?"

Toodles shrugged. "I suppose I do. Then again... Oh, never mind. Yes, I do find it fascinating."

"Ah, here's the main course," Henrietta smiled at the footman. "What do we have here? A mystery dish? We do love a mystery."

17

Halton House, the dining room

om frowned at the platter being offered. Helping himself to a portion, he sighed with relief. "It's fish. For a moment there, I thought I might have to wade through the awkwardness of tackling a fork I haven't used before. Thank heavens, I do know my fish fork from my..." He looked at the cutlery flanking his plate. "Well, the others, and there always seem to be so many of them."

Tom glanced at Evie who instantly understood his tactic. He was trying his best to divert everyone's attention.

But Henrietta would have none of it.

"The mystery person at church. That's what we were discussing. And then Henry was about to tell us about interviewing someone who might match our description."

Toodles laughed. "Description? We couldn't even decide if we'd seen a man or a woman."

Henrietta ignored her and continued, "That just goes to show you, Sara. I don't need a prompt card." Henrietta tittered. "This afternoon, Sara suggested writing prompt cards for me because, in her opinion, I tend to meander off topic. Then... oh, dear, I forgot what I'd been talking about. Never mind." She gave Tom a pointed look and then turned to Henry Evans. "You were saying?"

"One of the villagers I spoke with said he'd heard the stranger was staying at a pub nearby, in the next village. I drove out there and was told I could find him at Althea Rawlinson's house."

"Interesting. How did they know?" Sara asked.

"He made no secret of it, I suppose."

That was the first she'd heard about this. Evie looked at Tom but he was focused on his fish. Then again, they hadn't had the chance to speak with Henry Evans.

If Señor Lopes had made no secret of his where-abouts, then surely that meant he had nothing to hide.

On the other hand, a person with murder on their mind might pretend to have nothing to hide.

She picked up her glass of wine and took a pensive sip.

However, murderers were usually caught and that meant they made mistakes. They probably thought themselves superior and capable of getting away with... well, with murder.

Why would he let someone know where he could be found? Was it a sign of innocence?

"You mentioned his name earlier..." Henrietta looked at Henry Evans. "Mr. Lopes?"

"Señor Lopes."

"Señor Lopes," Henrietta repeated. "That sounds foreign. Is he Spanish?"

"I'm not sure. He doesn't have a strong accent."

"And what does Señor Lopes do? I'm rather intrigued by this mystery man, who is no longer a mystery man because we now know his name." Henrietta looked at Sara. "You should write the name down, Sara. It needs to go in the bottom row of our place cards."

"Should I do it now or wait until dinner is over?"

"When it suits you, of course. And try to do it without sarcasm. I'm just relieved we can finally put a name to the question mark." Turning to Henry Evans, Henrietta asked, "Is this Señor Lopes a suspect?"

"He is a person of interest. I have sent word to Scotland Yard. They will look into his background. If he has been in trouble with the police, I will soon know about it."

"Evangeline, why didn't you mention this to us?"

"I would have, Henrietta. Tom and I arrived rather late. We didn't wish to delay dinner so we both went up to change straightaway."

"I see. How considerate of you."

Henry turned to Evie. "Has Señor Lopes talked about the vicar at all?"

"Not that I recall."

"He's a man of few words," Tom offered.

Evie caught Edgar's attention and beckoned him over. "Edgar, could you please send word to Millicent to bring out my mourning clothes for tomorrow. If she knows about it now, she'll have ample time to do it."

"I believe Evangeline is trying to change the subject. Actually, Edgar, could you ask Millicent to let my maid know about the mourning clothes too, please?"

"Certainly, my lady."

"Oh, dear. Evangeline's tactic to divert our attention worked. I forgot what we were talking about." Henrietta held up her empty glass for a refill. "Thank you. I hope this will help jog my memory." She took a sip and then looked at Tom. "You met Señor Lopes today? Why would Henry assume Señor Lopes talked about the vicar? Did it come up in conversation?"

"Not that I recall."

"Interesting. Actually..." She turned to Henry Evans. "You said Señor Lopes is staying at the pub and left instructions saying he could be contacted at Althea Rawlinson's farm. Has he been a regular guest there?"

Evie coughed just as Henry Evans answered, "I believe so."

"I missed that," Sara said.

"Yes, I did too." Henrietta gave Henry Evans a raised eyebrow look.

Evie looked at Henry Evans and gave a discreet shake of her head. To his credit, he did not ask for an explanation.

Henry set down his fork and reached for his wine. "I'm sorry, what was the question?"

Henrietta looked up, her eyes looking to one side and then the other.

"The vegetables are delicious," Evie murmured.

Tom agreed. "Sweet peas are really sweet."

Leaning toward Toodles, Henrietta whispered, "What was the question?"

"You'll have to think of another one because I don't remember."

Henrietta tapped her finger on the table. "What does this Señor Lopes do?"

"I'm not entirely sure." Henry turned to Evie. "Has he mentioned what he does?"

"He's... He's a gentleman of means. Well, I assume he is because he said he'd stayed at the French Ambassador's house, and before that, he did some traveling." Evie looked at Tom.

"Yes, he mentioned New York and Paris."

"Is he a suspect?" Toodles demanded. "That's what I want to know."

"It's difficult to say at this point," Henry Evans admitted. "I just find his presence here highly unusual."

"And you say he's been a regular visitor. Has he been visiting Althea every day?"

"I didn't ask." Henry Evans looked at Evie. "Has he been there—"

Evie cut him off by coughing. "Oh, dear. My drink went down the wrong way."

Henrietta looked at her glass and then Evie's hand, which was nowhere near the glass.

Henrietta continued to study Evie as she said, "He sounds rather cosmopolitan. Why would he come to our little part of the world? You're right, his presence is rather unusual."

"Perhaps he wishes to have his portrait painted," Sara suggested. "After all, Althea is a portraitist."

"I am interested to see if he attends the funeral. It

should be an educational day. As for the family's uncharitable and uncouth behavior..." Henrietta glanced at Sara and Toodles. "It doesn't really come as a surprise. Not after what we learned today. Yes, indeed. We were very eager to share the news."

This time, Evie was the recipient of Henrietta's pointed look, which reached her with a degree of coolness.

Aha!

They'd come knocking at her door, eager to share their findings.

If she apologized, she knew she would be opening the proverbial can of worms.

"What did you discover, Henrietta?" Tom asked as a footman made his way around the table serving the dessert.

Henrietta clapped. "Peach Melba. My favorite. Heavens, this is such a treat." She looked up. "I'm sorry, what was the question?"

"Henrietta, you're playing hard to get," Sara chastised.

"Not at all. I am simply delighted by this dessert and I will have to do it justice by giving it my full attention."

"The line is broken," Toodles said. "Don't ask me what that means. All I know is that Henrietta was intrigued by it all and I assume that means something more now that Henry here has told us about the family and their uncouth behavior."

A mouthful of Peach Melba prevented Henrietta from stopping Toodles. When Evie saw her clutch a spoon, she thought she might throw it at Toodles.

"I'm sorry, did I speak out of turn?" Toodles cast her

gaze around the table. "Never mind what I just said. I'm sure Henrietta will explain it all to you."

The line is broken? Tom mouthed. Leaning in, he whispered, "What does that mean?"

Evie knew it had something to do with the line of succession. But whose line was Henrietta referring to?

When Henrietta finally savored the last spoonful of her dessert, everyone followed Evie's prompt and stood up.

Evie smiled at Tom. "We'll leave you gentlemen to your cigars and brandy."

"And miss hearing the explanation? Neither one of us smoke cigars." Sidling up to Evie, Tom whispered, "Why is she keeping us in suspense?"

"I think Henrietta is cross with me because, earlier, I ignored them when they came knocking at my door."

"So this is your doing?"

"Can we keep our finger pointing to possible suspects, please?"

They crossed the hall and entered the drawing room. Henrietta took her time deciding where she would sit.

Everyone, including Henry Evans, exchanged looks expressing curiosity and even concern.

"Is this going to help to identify a suspect, or better yet, the killer?" Tom asked.

Henrietta finally settled on a sofa and patted the space next to her, inviting someone to sit next to her.

Evie took the initiative, with Tom murmuring, "Brave."

Edgar walked in and handed Henrietta a book.

"Ah, thank you, Edgar. You are a treasure. We don't tell you often enough."

"Debrett's?" Henry Evans asked.

"Yes, when all else fails, always consult Debrett's." Looking for the entry she wanted, Henrietta smiled. "As I said, the line is broken and that explains the family's odd behavior. They simply were not born or bred to the task."

Tom looked puzzled.

"What Henrietta means," Evie said as she studied the entry, "is that there were several heirs over a short period of time. Direct heirs, with the last one dying at the Somme. So the title went to a distant relative."

"A very distant relative," Henrietta said. "The closer ones had also perished."

"I'm still in the dark," Tom said.

"The current earl was so far removed from the direct line, I'm sure he never expected to inherit."

"You see, Tom," Henrietta said, "not everyone is cut out to do their duty. Good behavior is taught and, we hope, learned. But some people are beyond the scope of learning correct behavior. Although, it's beyond me how anyone could fail to be polite."

Tom did not look impressed. "I was not born with a silver spoon in my mouth but I'd like to think I practice common sense."

"My dear, Tom. You are the exception."

"So," Evie drew in a deep breath. "The current earl and his heir are not polished. Does that make them suspects?"

"Indeed, it does." Henrietta nodded. "We have no idea what they are capable of. Actually, we do have some idea. They have no manners or common decency and now I find I have changed my mind. I don't really wish to meet them."

Tom shook his head. "No, I am still in the dark."

"We must simply be wary of them," Sara suggested. "And keep an open mind. Just because they have only stepped into the picture doesn't mean they are innocent of any involvement. They might have been working from afar."

Henry Evans tilted his head and frowned. "What reason could they possibly have for either murdering or engaging someone to murder one of their own."

Henrietta chortled. "You told us earlier they question his paternity." Shuddering, she added, "To think, this remark was made right in front of the Countess of Ester-brook. For all we know, she might be in the habit of encouraging such behavior."

"Henrietta is on the war path," Toodles declared.

"The unsavory alternative, my dear, is to find a killer among us."

Evie looked toward the door. For a moment, she wished Caro would burst in and distract them all.

"I'm going to toss and turn tonight," she mused. "I'm afraid Henrietta has seeded a disturbing thought and I won't be able to sleep easy until I unravel it."

18

———————

Another day, another suspect?

The next morning

*F*ortune favors the brave, Evie thought as she walked in to the dining room without hesitation. She had considered sending Millicent ahead to report on those present for breakfast but had changed her mind, mostly because she didn't wish to turn into the type of person who proceeded with caution.

Tom looked up from his newspaper. "You're not in mourning."

"I'll change later." Helping herself to some kippers and toast, she added, "I simply couldn't bear the idea of starting the day in a somber mood."

She sat down, poured herself some coffee, and waited until she'd taken her first sip to ask, "Where is Henry?"

"He received a telegram from Scotland Yard and left soon after." He smiled. "Without revealing the contents of the telegram."

"And you let him go?"

"What would you have had me do?"

"Next time, you should send for us."

"The Woodridge Countesses?"

"And Toodles. You mustn't forget about Toodles." Shaking her head, she stabbed her kipper with a fork, "Do you realize we're now going to spend the morning wondering what was in that telegram and everything we do will be affected by it."

"Why?"

"We might pursue someone already cleared by Scotland Yard."

"I see. You want to make sure our scant resources are properly allocated."

"Have you been reading the business section?"

Tom grinned.

"If time is a resource, then we are limited by what we can do before Henry decides to declare this case as unsolved or whatever the police does with unsolved case files."

"I'm sure they have a special filing cabinet for those." He studied her for a moment. "We've talked with everyone who might have had the opportunity to kill the vicar. Who's left?"

Evie smiled.

"Are you going to suspect the Earl of... what's his name?"

"Esterbrook and we haven't spoken with everyone. There's Peter McCraw."

"Elizabeth Handicott's fiancé?"

Evie nodded. "He seems to drive her everywhere."

"And?"

Evie tried to remember if she put sugar in her coffee. "She works in the next village. We know someone drives her back but we don't know how she gets there. He might drive her to work. At some point, he has to return."

"Oh, I see. On his way back here, he stopped by the field, killed the vicar, and then went about his business. What possible motive could he have?"

Jealousy? Betrayal? What could possibly drive someone to commit such a violent crime. He was engaged to marry Elizabeth Handicott. Had she made a habit of stopping at that particular field? Had the day she'd stopped at the field been the first time she'd gone there to collect flowers? Or had she made a habit of stopping at that particular field?

Sharing her thoughts, she added, "She must have been familiar with it."

"Are you about to suggest something happened during one of her visits?"

They had already painted a less than favorable picture of the vicar. Could she take it further and turn him into a grotesque creature?

"We saw the vicar emerge from the lane that runs alongside the field. For all we know, he had become a regular visitor there. The field might have been a new place of pilgrimage where he could commune with nature."

"Commune with nature and fight off the evil that dwelt within him?"

"You said that with a straight face."

Tom nodded. "How am I doing so far?"

"The edge of your eye just crinkled."

Tom sat back. "You're trying to suggest the vicar might have come across Elizabeth Handicott in the field and seduced her. Then, when her fiancé, Peter McCraw, found out about it, he decided to seek revenge."

Scant resources, scant information, Evie thought. They had been making the best of it by employing their active imaginations.

She knew the police worked with facts and evidence. If they found a footprint at the scene of a crime, they matched it to a shoe and then a person.

If they found a weapon, they looked for fingerprints. Their thought processes included taking reasonable steps.

Evie smiled at Tom.

"What?"

"I'm thinking about the investigative processes we employ."

"The ones more suited to an evening's entertainment?"

"Yes, those ones." She laughed. "Did we get carried away? I can't even remember how we entertained the idea of the vicar being a Casanova."

Tom raised his cup in a toast. "Deductive thinking, my dear. With a great deal of guesswork, wild presumption and speculation thrown in."

"Yes, I suppose there is madness in our process. But I believe it works."

"I doubt you'll find anyone brave enough to question it."

Evie hummed. "Has Elizabeth Handicott told us the truth, the whole truth and nothing but the truth?"

Tom shrugged. "I don't know. We haven't spoken with her."

"Precisely. We should speak with her."

Tom poured himself another cup of coffee. "Do you propose going to see them before or after the funeral service? Or do you think it might be better to attend the service, and observe everyone? The culprit might do something to give themselves away."

She knew the police would want more than an impression or a feeling they had about someone to justify taking them in for further questioning. "That's a very good idea. We will sift through the chaff."

"Isn't that what we've been doing? Determining who is good and identifying the potential for someone to be bad?"

Evie looked at Tom, her eyes filled with wonder. "I love the way you defined it all. It makes us sound quite clever."

His eyes softened but they didn't hide his amusement. "Here's a better idea. After the service, ask everyone to come back here."

"Everyone? The entire village?"

Tom laughed. "You don't need to take me literally. We could ask the vicar's family and... Yes, I see what you mean. We'll have to find a moment to approach Elizabeth Handicott and Peter McCraw."

"Not after the service because we'll have to hurry

back here." Evie twirled her fork around. "We might want to delay speaking to them until the afternoon."

Tom nodded in agreement. "That way, they'll think they're in the clear and they won't expect us. That is a sneaky tactic."

Looking up, Evie expected to find Edgar standing nearby, but she and Tom were alone in the dining room.

"Where is everyone?"

"I heard Edgar say something about overseeing the cleaning of the library. I think he's near breaking point."

Oh, dear.

They'd already had one person resigning from their post. Halton House could never survive without Edgar.

"I'm surprised the others haven't come down," Tom said.

"Henrietta must still be cross with me for not answering the knock at my door."

"Do you think she suspects?"

Evie didn't need Tom to explain.

"She might have put two and two together," he said.

"But why would we keep visits to Althea a secret?"

Tom snorted. "We did."

"Yes, but I'm sure she hasn't tied it in with... Oh, I don't know how her mind works."

Tom's face betrayed his astonishment. "How long have you known her?"

"Since 1910."

"And you still haven't worked out her character?"

"Henrietta is rather mysterious. She has secrets. I know she does. She has a particular way of smiling that always tells me she knows something I don't. The Victorians and Edwardians were not as virtuous and upright as everyone makes them out to be."

"Don't let her hear you say that. Remember, she's an accomplished swordswoman."

Edgar entered. His cheeks were flushed and his expression looked surprised.

"Edgar? Are you all right?"

"Perfectly fine, my lady. Although..." He looked down and appeared to realize he held a salver. "This just arrived for you, my lady."

Evie took the envelope. Opening it, she removed the single sheet of paper. "It's a note from Althea. Edgar, how did this get here?"

"She sent her butler, my lady. I believe he said his name was Withers."

Evie read the note and looked at Tom. "Henry just took Señor Lopes into custody. What do you think this means? The note doesn't include any other information, except she says Henry told her about the funeral service and she's interested in attending out of sheer curiosity, of course."

"It might all have something to do with the telegram he received. My guess is that Scotland Yard has dug up some information about Señor Lopes."

"Incriminating information."

He nodded. "I want to say he looked guilty but I know I'd be lying. He just looked indifferent and maybe confident."

"Edgar. There's a service for the vicar and we might ask everyone to return here."

Edgar brightened and inclined his head. "I shall make the necessary arrangements, my lady."

Evie turned her attention to her breakfast.

"Silence doesn't suit you."

She looked up. "Heavens, you think I'm entertaining a thought. Well, I'm not. Except... I can't believe no one has identified the woman with the jasmine scent."

"That is odd. Henry said a few people had mentioned seeing a stranger. Their description helped Henry identify Señor Lopes. Why did they notice him and not the woman?"

"If she wore a hat, it might have hidden her face." Evie groaned. "Are we supposed to treat every day as a possible crime scene?"

"What do you mean?"

"If we go to the pub for one of your favorite game pies, will we have to look at absolutely everyone there, just in case a crime is committed and we need to identify who was where?"

"When I go to the pub for my favorite pie, I only have eyes for the food... and you, of course."

Evie finished her coffee and set the cup down. "All this planning and plotting might be for nothing. Henry has taken Señor Lopes in for further questioning." She glanced at the envelope. "Althea only said Henry took him away. For all we know, he's been given enough proof to actually charge him. The case might actually be closed."

Tom laughed. "Edgar will be relieved to hear that. He can clear away the little village." Standing up, he added, "It's the strangest thing and I can't explain it, but I can't see Señor Lopes as the killer."

"We're still not clear on his reasons for wanting to come here."

"I don't have any trouble believing he wanted a change of scenery. Most people who come to England wish to see the countryside and experience the annual rituals such as hunting and shooting."

Evie could not have sounded less enthusiastic when she stood up and said, "I should go up and change. I suppose we need to attend the service even if the killer has been caught."

Shaking his head, Tom followed her out of the dining room. "Señor Lopes is not the killer."

As they crossed the hall and headed toward the stairs, they heard Millicent growl and holler, "Who moved the vicar?"

19

Halton House

$\mathcal{E}$ vie made her way down to the hall. Reaching the last step, she stopped and looked at the dowagers, Toodles, and Tom, all dressed in their mourning clothes. "Are we all ready?"

"Yes, absolutely." Henrietta looked around her. "We're all dressed appropriately. I'm just trying to decide if we look like a murder of crows or an unkindness of ravens."

Sara fidgeted with her hat. "I must say, black doesn't suit any of us."

Toodles gave the sleeve of her dress a tug. "I think this gown is about to see its last funeral service. It might be time for a new one."

Henrietta searched through her handbag and removed a lace handkerchief. "I'm sure there's no hurry."

Looking at Henrietta, Toodles raked her eyes from top

to bottom. "Are you sure? Death is not something you can really foretell. It can strike you at any moment."

Spluttering, Henrietta volleyed back, "Such unkindness. The raven himself is hoarse that croaks the fatal entrance of Duncan."

Toodles laughed. "I'm impressed but confused by the reference."

"The raven is really a raven. They are often the heralds of death, my dear. And I do not appreciate it. For your information, there is a long history of longevity in my family."

Evie interjected, "Are we ready?"

Tom took a step to the side and looked out the front door, which stood open. "Edmonds is waiting."

Herding everyone outside, Evie said, "We'll follow."

"We really should follow you, Evangeline. That would be the correct protocol."

"Two dowager countesses trumps one countess," Tom offered. Lowering his voice, he added, "I hope that doesn't give them leeway to do as they please."

"They're bound to interpret it in whatever way suits their purposes," Evie assured him and insisted, "We'll follow you."

They watched the Duesenberg drive away and couldn't help smiling at the sight of the dowagers and Toodles looking out the back window.

Tom chortled. "If we don't follow, they'll order Edmonds to stop and turn back."

Evie hurried to settle in. "I'm ready."

Putting the roadster into gear, Tom smiled at her. "Will we be sniffing our way in?"

"What?"

"The scent. We've yet to identify the mystery woman. She might attend the service."

"And you think she'll wear the same scent?" At one point, they had decided the scent had been a camouflage to disguise the wearer's usual scent.

"I don't know. That's why I'm wondering if we should sniff everyone."

"Thank you for not mentioning it within Henrietta's hearing. I can imagine her making her way along the pews, sniffing everyone who turned up for the vicar's funeral."

Heading to the church, Evie tried to picture the scene. Would the vicar's family put on a show by pretending to be somber and mourning the loss of one of their own?

They had already shown their true colors, their unrestrained behavior witnessed by Henry Evans.

He had only caught the tail end of remarks, perhaps not intended for his ears. But the true feelings had been expressed and the family's contempt for the Reverend Jeremiah Stamford had been blunt and unforgiving.

In Evie's opinion, their disdain for him explained why they hadn't arranged to bury him with the rest of their family.

Out of sight, out of mind.

A truly suspicious mind would entertain the possibility they had also ensured this outcome.

An unwanted family member, out of the way and no longer exposing them to scrutiny, even if their own behavior would eventually brand them as unsavory characters not welcomed in polite society.

Heavens. That would be truly wicked, she thought.

Evie closed her eyes and tried to rein in her thoughts.

With Nicholas' death, the line had been broken and the title had gone to someone who had never expected to inherit. Then, he too had died, leaving his young son to inherit.

Seth was such a sweet little boy, Evie couldn't imagine him growing up to be anything other than a perfect gentleman.

She glanced at Tom and instantly felt the reassurance she sought. She needn't worry. Seth would have all the guidance he'd need, from both of them.

They drove past the dower house. Evie saw a gardener clipping the hedges. That was one villager not attending the service. The leaky roof had been repaired long ago but Henrietta and Sara had chosen to remain at Halton House. Evie wouldn't have it any other way, especially with her granny still visiting.

"Where do you think we should leave the roadster?" Tom asked.

Evie looked ahead. There were several motor cars parked near the church, with people already making their way inside, although, she noticed quite a few hovering nearby talking.

What she wouldn't give to eavesdrop on those conversations, she thought.

"Somewhere out of sight might be a good idea." She checked her watch. "I think we're early."

"So are they." He gestured to the groups of people standing around in the church yard. "It must be curiosity. It's not every day the local vicar is murdered."

"Do you see anyone who looks like the earl and his family?"

"I think so. Right there by the front door."

Evie nibbled on the edge of her lip. "We still have time. The service is not due to start for another half hour."

"And you would like to do something, perhaps something underhanded?"

Evie winced. "Underhanded. That has too many negative connotations. I would prefer to say we are going to do something by stealth."

Tom's eyebrow hitched up. "Like thieves in the night?"

Rolling her eyes, she pointed to a side street. "Right there. The roadster should be safely out of sight there."

"While we do what?"

"While we go in and see if Mrs. Paterson is at the vicarage."

"And if someone from the uncouth family answers the door? What do we say?"

"We introduce ourselves and say we wished to offer our condolences. Actually, you should get us closer to the vicarage. It'll take us too long to walk around."

They headed along a side street, toward the back of the church. If Mrs. Leeds was still at home, she would notice them, but Evie couldn't imagine her mentioning it to the vicar's family.

Hurrying toward the front door, Evie had to stop herself from looking over her shoulder because that would make their attempts at discretion too obvious.

Tom knocked on the door and it opened straightaway.

"My lady." Mrs. Paterson excused herself saying she had been fixing her hat and being entirely too vain.

"May we come in, please? I take it the family have already made their way to the church."

Mrs. Paterson nodded and stepped aside to let them

in. "Mrs. Leeds was right all along. You are investigating the case."

"We're showing an interest, Mrs. Paterson."

"How can I help, my lady?"

"The vicar's personal effects. Have they been packed?"

"I was going to do that, thinking the family wished to take it all with them this afternoon when they leave, but I've been asked to get rid of everything."

"Have you looked through his personal possessions? Books? Letters?"

Mrs. Paterson stepped back. "I would never."

"Did he have any private letters?"

"No."

"What about something that looked odd? Out of place? Something like a lace handkerchief or some sort of keepsake." The vicar had gone to that field to meet someone. A clandestine meeting. Tom had mentioned it the first time they had encountered the vicar on the road and Evie was inclined to agree.

Mrs. Paterson shook her head. "While I did not scrutinize his belonging, I did handle everything as I was putting it all away. I assure you, my lady, I did not find anything unusual."

Evie looked around the hallway. The door to his study was open. Peering inside, she saw that it had already been cleared of anything that might have been personal.

"Flowers. I don't see any vases of flowers." She imagined the vicar expressing a fondness for jasmine and asking Mrs. Paterson to make sure to include some in the arrangements.

"He didn't care for flowers. Although..."

"Yes?"

"I found something I thought he might have brought back from his... well, from wherever he went."

"What was it?"

"A sprig of jasmine. It was quite wilted. I found it pressed inside a book."

Jasmine.

They thanked Mrs. Paterson and Evie apologized for keeping her.

Stepping outside, they watched her lock up and hurry to the church.

Evie and Tom followed. This time, they didn't worry about being seen because they knew their excuse of wanting to offer their condolences would sound credible.

"What was that about?" Tom asked.

"I'm thinking of all my personal possessions, including the pieces of paper with notes I've inserted in some books in the library. When my time comes, the house will pass on to someone else and my possessions will probably be put in boxes and stored in the attic for some future countess to discover and, most likely, discard. There are letters and some journals, my diaries with appointments. He left no trace of him behind. I find that sad."

"Yes, but what do you make of the jasmine Mrs. Paterson found pressed in the book."

"We might be looking for someone named Jasmin." Evie's gaze dropped to the ground. "Did the woman with the jasmine scent give it to him?"

"Most likely but we haven't identified her." Tom looked into the distance. "Do you realize what this means?"

"Are you about to say our light entertainment actually

yielded results?" They had been quick to form opinions about the vicar, casting him in an unflattering light. Evie laughed. "I wouldn't be so quick to crow. He might have been trying to save a lost soul."

Tom frowned. After a moment, he smiled. "Oh, I get it."

"What?"

"The crowing reference."

They turned into the path leading to the church.

"Do you see Henry?" It was nearly time for the service to start, but she couldn't see anyone hurrying inside. People were still gathered in groups, milling about, talking and looking around them.

"Do you think they're wondering if there is a killer among us?" Evie asked.

"That would be my guess. It's what we're doing."

Yes and, Evie thought, their main concern would actually be the fact the killer hadn't been apprehended. She didn't want to think about anyone looking at their neighbors and doubting their integrity.

"I don't see Henry. Where could he be?"

"Interrogating his suspect."

"I wish you wouldn't smile when you say that."

Tom nudged his head toward the entrance. "Time to introduce yourself."

She saw the group of people congregated near the entrance and decided the oldest of them had to be the Earl of Esterbrook. "He lacks presence."

"Really? That's odd. He looks like an earl."

"Just because you wear the most impressive suit doesn't mean you are the most impressive man." The earl stood with his back erect and his chin lifted and didn't appear to meet anyone's gaze. "I'll bet anything he looks down his nose at me."

Her husband, Nicholas, had been so sweet natured and friendly to everyone, regardless of their station in life. That had been the first trait she'd admired in him.

Veritas et integritas.

"What?" Tom asked.

"Truth and integrity. The Woodridge family motto."

As they drew closer, Tom said, "Yes, you're right. There's something not quite right with him. He's trying too hard."

"You don't *tell* people you are good, you *show* them by your good deeds," Evie suggested.

His wife was no better. She had a tight smile and a sharp gaze and the look of someone who'd rather be anywhere but here.

Evie stepped forward, introduced herself and Tom and offered her condolences.

"Yes, a dreadful loss, and an inconvenience for the village, I'm sure." The earl broke eye contact and checked his watch. Looking at his wife, he said, "I suppose you should go in now."

Evie turned her attention to the younger man standing next to the earl. The son bore a faint resemblance to his father. Same light brown hair, long nose, broad shoulders, and heavy build. Evie could understand why the vicar's paternity might be brought into question. He'd had light colored hair and had been quite slim.

As they moved away and toward the entrance, Tom leaned in and whispered, "If we are to believe our theory about the vicar being a Casanova, we would have to suspect him of bringing his family into disrepute, which would give his family a reason to benefit from his death." Tom grinned. "The more I think about it, the more I like the idea."

"Especially now that you've met them." Evie stepped inside and shivered. Henrietta had been right. The temperature did drop inside the church. "I want to say we should be alert and observe everything and everyone but we should really be sniffing."

Gesturing to the earl's wife walking ahead of them, Tom whispered, "Did you smell her?"

Belatedly, Evie realized they had missed their opportunity to mingle with everyone before coming inside. If only she hadn't thought of going to the vicarage. Although, they had walked away with a tidbit of information, which might prove useful.

Her gaze skated from one side of the church to the other, taking in as much as she could, even as they walked up to the front pew.

The vicar's mother took her place on the left front pew. As she sat down, a woman looked up and greeted her.

Evie gaped.

Petronella Gladstone.

She must have made quite an impression on the family to have been invited to sit with them.

As she watched the two women engage in a murmured conversation, Evie tried to bring to mind the place cards with the parishioners' names, but drew a blank. She assumed everyone had moved down one pew to make way for the family.

"Where is Henry?" she whispered.

"Probably hovering somewhere near the back."

"Are you telling me we walked in and missed looking at everyone sitting in the back pews again? I really need to hone my observation skills, as well as my focus."

"You mustn't be so hard on yourself. When you're distracted, you notice other things."

They reached the front pew and took their places next to the dowagers and Toodles.

"Where have you been?" Henrietta demanded. "We thought you were right behind us. Did you speak with them?"

Evie assumed Henrietta was referring to the vicar's family. "Only briefly."

"You should know, Toodles insisted on sitting at the end. She refuses to participate in disciplining me with elbow jabs. I have no idea what she is talking about."

"No, nor do I."

Henrietta stifled a yelp. Turning to Sara, she demanded, "What was that for?"

"Did you tell her?"

"Tell her what?"

"About the jasmine scent."

"Oh, yes." Henrietta turned to Evie. "We definitely caught a whiff of jasmine."

Evie swiveled toward Henrietta. "Where? When?"

"We noticed it as we were walking in. There is a dispute as to whether it came from the right side or the left side of the church. However, someone here is definitely wearing it."

Evie turned to Tom. "Did you hear that?"

"Just barely and, no, I did not pick up on the scent. It might have something to do with the fact that I'm not exactly acquainted with it."

Evie glanced over her shoulder. "Oh, good heavens. I forgot all about Althea. Did you see her?"

Tom shook his head, and murmured, "Kerfuffle."

"What did Tom say?" Henrietta demanded, but did not wait for a response. "Oh, have you seen the vicar?"

"I'm sure the procession will begin soon," Evie assured her and added, "They're bound to have selected a nice coffin."

"Not that vicar. The new one."

It took Evie a moment to realize that, of course, there would be a new vicar to deliver the service.

"They called him in from the next village. I hear he loves his singing. Mrs. Hammond just received her signal," Henrietta whispered as the church organist began playing the opening hymn.

A wave of questions swept through the church.

"Which page?"

"Which hymn?"

One by one, they searched through their hymn books, found their place, and sang, but their efforts were drowned out by the vicar's booming voice.

The bare casket was viewed with wide-eyed amazement.

The absence of a wreath was met with puzzlement.

A parishioner stepped up for the first reading.

Turning slightly, Evie strained to see what was going on around her.

The brief silence following the reading, was broken by a hearty rendition of *The Lord's My Shepherd*.

At the start of the second reading, Henrietta shuddered.

"*Death is nothing at all. I have only slipped away into the next room...*"

Tom leaned back and nudged Evie. Taking it as a prompt, she glanced at the vicar's family and saw Petronella Gladstone sitting next to the earl's son, a handkerchief raised to her eye.

Deciding the vicar was doing a fine job, Evie gave up trying to contribute to the singing and only mouthed the words to the next hymn.

The order of service proceeded without a glitch, the solemn occasion reaching the end as the vicar delivered the blessing.

"*He has achieved success who has lived well, laughed often and loved much: who has enjoyed the trust of pure women...*"

Henrietta's unladylike snort did not go unnoticed.

The procession made its way out of the church, with the family filing out and, to Evie's surprise, joined by Petronella Gladstone.

"Who is that young woman?" Sara asked.

Evie offered a brief explanation, including how they had met, but her thoughts were focused on finding Althea.

"There's Henry." Tom signaled to the entrance. "He's waiting for us."

Instead of following the procession out, Evie and Tom slowed their steps, and as the congregation emptied the church, they reached him.

"Henry, we've been looking for you."

Nodding, Henry Evans gestured to the door. "We should follow them."

Lowering her voice, Evie asked, "What happened? We heard you took Señor Lopes into custody."

"I received word from Scotland Yard and had some questions for Señor Lopes."

"About?"

"Mostly about his first meeting with the Reverend Jeremiah Stamford, but also about his sister, Helena Lopes."

So they had met. "Did they meet in London?"

Henry Evans nodded. "At *The Ritz*, of all places. It seems the vicar enjoyed living the high life."

"And Helena Lopes?" Evie asked, her tone suggestive.

"He tried to sweet talk her into running away with him. Enter Señor Lopes. He put a stop to it. However, he was rather late and the vicar had already..." Henry appeared to search for the rights words. "Seduced? No, I'm going to say cultivated. Or, rather, he was priming Helena Lopes for seduction."

"Good heavens. What happened?"

"Señor Lopes says he warned him off."

"Did he come here to drive the message home?"

"He wanted to show the vicar how capable he was of tracking him down. Apparently, there had been a further attempt to contact his sister."

"But he didn't kill the vicar." Tom had already expressed his thoughts on the matter and Evie agreed with him. Neither one thought Señor Lopes would be capable of something so obvious.

"His whereabouts can actually be confirmed. So I have cleared him of all suspicion."

"Was he really a suspect?"

"Oh, yes. Absolutely." Henry tipped his hat back. "Truth be known, I'm at a loss now."

They all cast their gazes around the church yard.

Most people had congregated around the grave, while a few maintained a respectful distance.

"There you are."

Evie and Tom turned to see Althea hurrying toward them, her brother Theodore trailing behind her.

"Oh, I told Theo we'd be late and we are. What did we miss?" She looked at Henry Evans. "And is Señor Lopes behind bars?"

"No, he's not." Henry Evans stepped away and joined Theo and Tom.

"Is that them?"

"The vicar's family? Yes."

"Oh, and what's Petronella doing cozying up to that young man?" Althea smiled. "I honestly don't understand why she is still single. She certainly tries hard enough."

"She went to meet the family as soon as they arrived." Evie frowned. "I wonder how she knew."

"Maybe she has a spy in the village, someone to keep an eye out for prospective husbands." Althea tilted her head from side to side. "There's a lot you can tell by watching how people behave at a funeral. I only see one person with their head bowed."

"Who?"

"That young woman..." Althea broke off and laughed lightly. "I was about to say the woman in black but everyone is dressed in black. I rushed and could only find dark gray. Anyhow, the man next to her is wearing a brown coat."

Evie located them. "Peter McCraw and Elizabeth Handicott. They're engaged."

"She must be distraught by the experience."

"Finding the vicar?" She hadn't looked in any way

distraught when she'd seen her the previous day visiting Mrs. Higgins to show her the flowers she had collected.

Flowers.

"Henrietta said someone wore a jasmine fragrance." Evie searched for the dowager and saw her approaching the Stamford family. "Would you excuse me for a moment." Evie hurried away and headed back inside the church.

Her steps echoed in the now empty church.

She knew where Henrietta had picked up the jasmine scent. At least, she thought she knew.

Turning toward the left, she walked to the pillar which had a stand next to it. On the stand, there was a large vase with flowers. A similar one had been placed on the opposite side. She studied the sumptuous display and found what she'd been looking for. She caught the scent before she saw the flowers.

Jasmine.

Walking out of the church, she saw Tom looking over his shoulder. When he saw her, he took a step toward her but Evie was already moving. She'd spotted Mrs. Leeds about to cross the street.

As Evie hurried toward her, she beckoned for Tom to join her. She need not have bothered because he was already by her side.

"What's happened?" he asked.

"There was jasmine in the flower arrangements." Evie called out. "Mrs. Leeds."

Thankfully, she stopped and turned. "My lady?"

"Mrs. Leeds. I wanted to ask you about the flowers. I take it you provided the display for the service?"

"I did, yes."

"They are quite beautiful, as always. But I'm confused."

"Why is that, my lady?"

"You put jasmine in and I thought you didn't care for the scent."

"No, not really. That is, not a pungent one. There's a difference."

"Is there?"

"Yes, the flowers in my displays give out a hint of fragrance. Whereas, the scent I found offensive came out of a bottle and the person had worn too much."

"Do you normally include jasmine in your displays? Forgive me, but I never noticed."

Mrs. Leeds smiled. "No, I don't have jasmine in my garden. I found those at my front door this morning with a note saying they had been the vicar's favorite flowers."

"A note? Was it signed?"

Mrs. Leeds frowned. She then opened her handbag and retrieved a piece of paper. "I was going to show it to Mrs. Higgins. However, now that I think about it, I should have shown it to you or the detective."

"May I see it?"

Mrs. Leeds handed her the note.

"Do you mind if I show it to the detective?"

Mrs. Leeds gave a tentative nod. "Am I in trouble?"

If someone had left the jasmine outside the vicarage door, Mrs. Leeds would have seen them. But the person had chosen to leave them at her doorstep. When and why?

She had to ask. "You didn't see who it was that left the flowers?"

"I wish I had. What do they mean? Oh, is this about the scent worn by that woman?"

"It might be."

She thanked Mrs. Leeds and returned to the church with Tom saying, "That looks, without a doubt, suspicious."

"If I had to guess, I'd say the person who wore the scent wishes to throw us off the scent."

20

*E*vie wished she could identify the writing on the note.

Tom nudged her. "Elizabeth Handicott and her fiancé are headed this way. Do you still wish to speak with them?"

She couldn't remember why she'd wanted to speak with either one. At that moment, she could only think about the note and the jasmine.

Tom greeted them.

Evie remembered Althea mentioning the way Elizabeth Handicott had bowed her head.

"This must have been difficult for you."

"It was a shock, my lady. I'm surprised his family didn't ask to speak with me. I thought they might have been curious to know how he'd been found. Then again, I suppose the police told them all about it."

Evie didn't think they would care enough to ask.

By the sounds of it, they had done their duty and wished to be on their way.

She was about to offer some comforting words when Elizabeth Handicott retrieved a handkerchief from her pocket and pressed it lightly against the corner of her eye.

The scent of jasmine wafted toward her.

Tom's hand cupped her elbow and he drew her back.

"Well, we must be on our way. Actually, this might not be the most appropriate time, however, I wished to congratulate you both on your upcoming marriage."

The couple exchanged a look filled with warmth. "We are both looking forward to it, my lady."

Evie dug inside her handbag and brought out her pen and notebook. Handing them to Elizabeth, she asked, "I wonder if you wouldn't mind noting down your address. We would love to send something on the day."

Although surprised, Elizabeth Handicott obliged her.

Taking the notebook and pen back, Evie thanked her.

As they walked away, Tom murmured, "Brilliant. Well done, Countess."

She looked down at the note Mrs. Leeds had given her just as Henrietta hurried toward them.

"Evangeline. That man might be your social equal but he fails to show it at every turn. Can you believe it? He was so discourteous." Henrietta waved her hand. "Brushed me aside, dismissed me when I was in the middle of offering my condolences, and the wife is not better. As for the son." Henrietta looked heavenward. "He displayed a noticeable sneer."

Evie looked around but did not see the Stamfords. "Have they left?"

"And thank goodness for that." She pointed at the road and a fancy motor car. "Yes, there they go. I must say that young woman with them was equally rude. Althea tells me you know her."

"I met her the one time, Henrietta."

"Please tell me you will not be pursuing her acquaintance. Good riddance, I say... Look, there she goes, chasing after them."

Evie turned and saw the young woman driving by in a roadster. "Impressive. Althea told me her father keeps her on a tight leash. He must have a soft spot for her. Well, it's all over now, Henrietta. They've left." And she hadn't had the opportunity to invite them back to the house.

They joined the others and as they walked back, Evie held up the note Mrs. Leeds had given her and compared it to the address Elizabeth Handicott had written down.

"Well?" Tom asked.

Evie showed him the note and notebook.

"What is this? What are you looking at?" Henrietta asked.

Tom explained about the writing and the jasmine in the flower display.

"Are you saying that's what we smelled?"

"Most likely, Henrietta."

They reached the others and Evie extended an invitation to join them back at the house.

"Evangeline has just discovered a new part of the puzzle." Henrietta went on to explain the rest.

When she finished, Toodles asked, "Birdie? Is that the real version or Henrietta's exaggerated version?"

Smiling, Evie assured her, "Henrietta did very well. She actually gave you a brief summary."

"Brevity can also be quite dramatic, my dear."

Henry Evans compared the writing styles. "They are quite different."

"Her handkerchief smelled of jasmine. For a wild moment, I thought I'd stumbled on something."

"Interesting. I've spoken with her and I don't recall her wearing a scent." He looked into the distance. "I think I might have another word with her."

"I suppose we should head back to the house. I'd actually asked Edgar to organize refreshments."

"I am glad they left before you could invite them, Evangeline. They truly are quite disagreeable. People like that give the rest of us a bad name."

Tom laughed. "Henrietta, who has given you a bad name?"

"They. *They*." Henrietta waved her hand about. "Everyone who thinks we have no right to exist."

Evie patted Henrietta on her arm. Before she could bring up the French Revolution, she again suggested they all return to Halton House.

"What's the hurry?" Tom asked as they walked back to the roadster.

She slowed down. "I geared myself to escape Henrietta."

When they reached the roadster and she settled in the passenger seat, she brought out the piece of paper again. "I won't lie. I'm disappointed the writing didn't match. Although, I'm relieved for Elizabeth Handicott."

"The murderer is still at large."

"Yes, and now the vicar has been laid to rest, I fear the trail will go cold." Evie laughed. "Just listen to me. I'm talking like a detective straight out of a book."

"I noticed Señor Lopes did not attend the service. I

would have thought he'd be keen to seen him buried. We know more about him now than we did before and now he is more of a puzzle than he was when we first met him."

Evie looked at Tom. "That's an interesting observation. Henry didn't say anything about Señor Lopes packing his bags and moving on. He came here to make sure the vicar stayed away from his sister. Why is he still here?"

"That's a good question."

Evie spent the rest of the drive back thinking about it but did not manage to come up with a reasonable explanation.

Driving up to the house, they saw Edgar walking across the front lawn with Holmes dashing around him.

Seeing them, Edgar leaned down and scooped Holmes up.

Tom brought the motor car to a stop. "If only we could train Holmes to sniff out murders. Our job would be that much easier."

Edgar hurried to open the passenger door for Evie. "My lady. I trust the service went well."

"As well as can be expected, Edgar."

"Everything is set up in the drawing room, my lady."

"Thank you, Edgar. I hope Holmes wasn't too much trouble." Taking him from Edgar, Evie scratched his chin.

"Master Holmes will always do as he pleases. That is his nature."

They headed inside with Tom saying, "Why do I feel we've missed something obvious?"

"That's because we have, I'm sure of it. Don't worry, it will come to us."

They were soon joined by Althea and her brother, Theodore, who confided in Tom, "I made sure we'd be late for the service. Althea doesn't seem to understand I deal with death for a living. I have no desire to experience any of it during my vacation."

"I'm sorry to say you'll be hearing more about it all. It's all we can talk about."

Theodore shook his head. "You might need to face the possibility the case won't be solved."

"Yes, we've already discussed it. Evie doesn't care for unanswered questions."

The dowagers and Toodles joined them.

"A cup of tea should fix me right up," Henrietta said. "That man gave me the chills."

"Henrietta, I hope you're not having a relapse."

"No, no. It's that horrid man and his family."

"Out of sight, Henrietta, out of mind. Sara and I heard that young woman inviting them all back to her house."

"Which young woman?"

"The one who sat with them."

"Petronella Gladstone?" Althea asked. "She looked keen enough. I think she's set her sights on the heir."

Gain. The word bounced around her mind.

Lost in her thoughts, Evie poured herself a cup of tea and walked to the window. "Some criminals return to the scene of the crime and pretend to be spectators," she whispered. That had been the constable's explanation for arresting Edmonds.

Henry Evans had told them the vicar's wallet had been taken. Had that been on purpose to make the incident look like a robbery gone wrong?

Her thoughts were momentarily scattered by Henrietta's conversation.

"She's welcome to the lot of them," Henrietta declared. "Although, even with the scarcity of fish in the sea, I'm sure she could do better."

"She's tried," Althea assured her. "In fact, she was recently presented. She missed out on her coming out because of the war and then her mother fell ill, so there were no trips to town. This year, she was determined to be presented." Shrugging, she added, "I didn't see her. Then again, there were quite a number of people being presented over several days."

Taking a sip of her tea, Evie remembered they had already discussed motive and no one had been able to come up with anything. Then, there was the theory based on the vicar's habit of staying out until late.

"Gain," she murmured.

"Who would have the most to gain from the vicar's death?" Tom asked as he came to stand beside her.

"Yes."

"He wasn't the heir. Otherwise, I'm sure Henrietta would be quite happy to pin the murder on the earl's son."

"Petronella Gladstone only just met the family and now she's invited them back to her house."

Hearing her, Althea set her teacup down and joined them. "The prospect of acquiring a title would be quite an incentive for her."

"She drives an impressive motor car," Tom observed.

"She must have borrowed it from her father. Petronella is a serious walker. It's how she manages to stay slim."

"I hope you and Theodore will join us for luncheon," Evie invited.

"We'd be delighted to."

"What am I delighting in?" Theodore Rawlinson asked as he joined them by the window.

"We've been invited to luncheon."

He lifted his cup to his lips. "I'll drink to that. Anything that keeps me away from home and the possibility of Señor Lopes returning to give you your lessons. You must know you've become quite the expert Tango dancers."

One by one, the dowagers and Toodles approached them.

"What's this I hear about Tango dancing?"

Smiling, Theodore explained, "They've been perfecting their Tango. Specifically, the Argentine Tango. Apparently, there is a difference to what everyone else dances. Señor Lopes is an expert."

Neither Evie nor Tom had been able to act quickly enough to stop Theodore Rawlinson from revealing their secret.

"And this has been going on at your house?" Henrietta asked.

Evie's cup rattled on its saucer. "Well, I must say, as far as funeral services go, that was... notable. You missed seeing your vicar in action."

"The Reverend John Peters was here?" Althea asked.

"Yes, and he brought his booming voice."

Henrietta interjected, "You were about to tell us how long these Tango dancing lessons have been going on for."

"Oh, I'm not really sure. You see, I've only just arrived." Theodore turned to his sister.

"Henrietta." Evie sighed. "It was meant to be a surprise."

Henrietta lifted her chin. "In that case, congratulations, you have succeeded in surprising us. When exactly were you going to reveal your secret to us?"

"We hadn't decided. Tom and I were merely working hard to become proficient."

"I suppose this went on while we were on our deathbeds."

"Not quite. You had all, more or less, recovered by then." Looking up, Evie saw Henry Evans walking in. "Please tell me that is a look of triumph."

"This conversation is not over," Henrietta murmured.

Evie poured him a cup of tea and handed it to him. "Did you manage to talk to Elizabeth Handicott?"

"Yes. Her entire day can be accounted for, we already knew that, but I wanted to ask her about the jasmine scent."

Having recovered from what she would no doubt term as a betrayal, Henrietta asked, "And what did she have to say for herself?"

"It was a gift. She doesn't know who sent it and she's only used it on her handkerchief."

"This can't be a coincidence. Someone left jasmine for Mrs. Leeds to use on the flower arrangements. And now you say Elizabeth Handicott received the jasmine scent and doesn't know who sent it." Nodding, Evie walked out of the drawing room and headed to the library.

Everyone else followed.

Evie went straight to the place cards.

Henrietta went to stand next to her. "As Elizabeth Handicott appears to be a person of interest, I should tell you she sat on the right-hand side of the church."

"How do you know?"

"I asked her but, I must admit, when I spoke to her, I did not pick up the jasmine scent."

"It was on her handkerchief." Evie resumed thinking about gain. "Gain as a motive. Mrs. Paterson, the vicar's housekeeper, found a sprig of jasmine pressed in one of his books. It looked like a keepsake. Can we assume he was seeing someone?"

"Evangeline, we've been thinking that from the start."

"Yes, but I suspect it might have been serious. And now I'm wondering about the woman's reaction when she learned the vicar was a second son. Where there is a second son, there is an heir. A far better prospect."

Tom nodded and stepped forward. "Gain by getting the vicar out of the way. If, when she heard about the heir she was already involved with the vicar, it would all become awkward."

"Exactly. More so if the vicar was in love with the woman." Evie swung away. "We know he drove out to meet with Margaret Dalgety. She'd met him and had become infatuated with him. Of course, we don't know the whole story. The vicar might have led her on. We'll never really know the truth. However, it was Sunday and he was going to meet with his beloved but, first, he had to make sure there were no misunderstandings to interfere."

Althea cleared her throat. "Are you actually saying what I think you're saying?"

Henrietta looked at Althea and then at Evie. "One of you will have to spell it out."

"Petronella Gladstone."

"What about her? Oh, oh heavens. She drove off with the heir." Henrietta pressed her hand to her throat. Looking toward the door, she shook her head. "My dear, Edgar is standing at the door. Luncheon is about to be served. You might have waited until we'd finished to reveal this. Now Henry will need to dash off and subject the girl to an interrogation until he wrenches the truth out of her, and then arrest her and we'll all be here sitting on the edge of our seats, waiting to hear all about it."

Two weeks later

"It's comforting to know the new vicar comes highly recommended," Henrietta whispered. "He has a wife and they've been happily married for twenty years. His eyes twinkle when he smiles. That's always a good sign, I'm sure of it."

"What would you have done if he had failed to meet your standards?" Sara asked. "Sent him back?"

"Yes, with an explanation saying he wasn't a good fit. Of course, I would have had the decency to allow a decent amount of time to elapse before doing so. After all, everyone deserves a sporting chance."

"How very magnanimous of you."

"My dear, don't think I failed to notice the underlying sarcasm. If we have to sit and listen to the man every Sunday, we must be allowed to expect satisfaction."

Toodles leaned in and whispered, "Birdie, they're at it again. What are you going to do about it?"

Evie rolled her eyes and prayed for the service to be over.

"This one has a pleasant voice," Henrietta continued. "Don't you think so? Yes, he will do just fine. He's coming to dinner tonight. We should all be on our best behavior."

"*I publish the Banns of marriage between Tom Winchester of Woodridge and the Countess of Woodridge from Woodridge. If any of you know cause or just impediment...*"

"It just seems odd that..."

"What?" Sara asked.

"Oh, never mind. I'm sure it's nothing."

"It must be something if you thought about it."

"What did he just say?"

"I think he's reading the banns."

"Again? He's only just married all those people and now there are more. At least he'll be kept busy with happy occasions. I, for one, don't intend giving him my business for quite some time. I must say, he will do just fine. You should make sure he has a haircut. I wouldn't want him looking scruffy on my final goodbye. But, as I said, I still have a few good years left in me."

Evie didn't know which way to look. As soon as the service ended, she made her way out. Offering a warm smile, she said, "Lovely service," and, taking hold of Tom's arm, hurried to the roadster. "A long drive, please."

Tom looked at his watch. "You seem to forget Henry and Caro are coming for luncheon."

Yes, for the briefest moment, she had forgotten. "He must be pleased to have wrapped up the case."

"All thanks to you. I believe he will be eating humble

pie. You should have thought of including that on the menu."

Evie drew in a deep breath.

She didn't want to think about the outcome of Henry's investigation. Not today.

The banns had finally been read.

In a few weeks, she would finally walk down the aisle. The invitations had been sent out. Everyone at Halton House was buzzing with excitement. Rooms were being readied for all the guests.

"Correct me if I'm wrong, I have the feeling Henrietta talked right through the reading of the banns."

"She did. Any minute now, she will find out and we'll never hear the end of it."

"I told you we should have made the announcement at dinner but you insisted they should hear it at church."

Evie grinned. "It was rather wicked of me. In my defense, I thought it would be quaint."

No, she didn't want to think about the outcome of the investigation but her mind was already flooding with everything she knew.

She closed her eyes and was instantly flung back to two weeks before.

Soon after their discussion, Henry Evans had driven out to the Gladstone house and had taken Petronella Gladstone in for questioning.

The evidence had been circumstantial but, in the end, Henry's perseverance had won the day. She had even confessed to attending Sunday service and using the heavy scent as a disguise.

Evie glanced at the landscape around her.

Justice had been served but she couldn't help feeling

sorry for the young woman. If only she had been happy enough to settle for the vicar. Also, she'd never met Sir George Gladstone. The poor man had lost his wife and now he'd lost his daughter.

Evie found the murder tragic on too many levels to count.

"No sign of Edgar. All must be well," Tom mused.

"Edgar has other things to do today."

"What do you mean?"

"He and Millicent have gone on a picnic." Evie smiled and hoped all went well for Millicent who had been practicing her poem until she learned it by heart.

Shifting, she leaned and rested her head on Tom's shoulder. "Are you finally going to tell me?"

"Tell you what?"

"Where we're going on our honeymoon."

"Oh, that... Well, I guess you'll just have to wait until we get there."

***

Printed in Great Britain
by Amazon